Iliya Englin

NO EVIL REIGNS
FOREVER

A novel?

THIS BOOK IS DEDICATED TO THE MILLIONS WHO FOUGHT MARXISM AS LONG AS ITS SHADOW DARKENED THE WORLD:

YOUR DEEDS MAY REMAIN UNKNOWN.

YOU ARE REVILED BY THOSE WHOSE FUTURE YOU FOUGHT TO PROTECT.

DESPITE DESPERATE EFFORTS MANY NATIONS REMAIN IN ENEMY HANDS.

BUT YOUR HEARTS AND MINDS WERE TRUE. YOU DID WHAT WAS RIGHT WHEN OTHERS SOLD OUT AND SURRENDERED.

TO THOSE STILL FIGHTING - I SALUTE YOU, BROTHERS IN ARMS.

REMEMBER, IN YOUR THANKLESS QUEST:

NO EVIL REIGNS FOREVER.

Some distance into the foothills of Victorian Alps a thankless gravel road wound through sparse vegetation.

One barely noticeable dirt track branched into the bush and meandered past a small property with electric fencing. A practised eye would soon spot an incongruity - despite expensive, well-maintained barriers, the property showed no evidence of recent grazing.

Weeds and even young trees reached up from the dry soil with not a single piece of farm machinery in sight. A single iron-clad dwelling painted olive green was situated in a clump of taller vegetation. A grave fire risk in this arid terrain, bushy trees made the building almost invisible from the road.

One had to drive through the heavy gate and some distance into the property to marvel how a sunrise of fading summer lit the windows of the shack a deep mauve colour.

A man stood on the veranda and stared into the hills, squinting in the sun. He was alone with his despair that day, pain being in no hurry to revisit his much-seared soul. He had long lost count of sunrises that drifted past his hiding place in the serene silence of the hills.

Like all Russian defectors, he was a breathing corpse, a faded silhouette of former self. Burning anger and smouldering resentment were drained years before, and he became what any Russian eventually becomes once separated from his culture - alien flotsam in a foreign sea, bearing the agony of isolation in sullen silence.

Driven beyond endurance by tension and danger, he sought shelter among lazy and sated people. His defection never became public - a secret so well guarded by his hosts that he was still alive all these years later. Yet as soon as immediate danger subsided, he knew there would be no inner peace. Not then, not later, not ever.

He swapped his dangerous life for a vacuum, and bitter irony lay in realization that he miscalculated. He should not have run - just a few more years, and his country will be run by men like himself.

When he read about the changes in Russia, his mood turned black with impotent anger. Ambition mingled with genuine patriotism, they boiled his blood as he read about the misrule of his land.

Yet there was no doubt that in due course a different breed of men would rise amid the meaningless debauchery that festered on the bloated corpse of the Soviet empire. It was certain that any time soon real leaders will take hold of Russia, and they will forge her resurrection with steel tempered in blood.

He seethed with realization that he would never be one of these saviours. He was a traitor, marked for eternal contempt by his countrymen - not to mention that his personal expertise was likely to cause him a lot of trouble. Some would want him silenced, and others would seek to exploit his knowledge - neither scenario being conducive to a long life.

In any case, there was no doubt as to what would happen if the current government learned of his location, and fear of that was the only emotion that rivalled his frustration. For a year he was safely hidden in this wasteland, his identity known only to a handful of elderly men, but there were times when suspended animation hurt more than a noose around his throat.

He seldom ventured out, making monthly trips to the nearest town where he exchanged little more than muted greetings with shopkeepers. They knew him as Hörst Meister, a pseudonym he could support with the competent German he acquired in youth. No one knew what he did and no one asked. Times were hard, and rural folk had plenty of other things to worry about.

He once worked in a small cheese factory in the district, making modest use of his expertise with guilty pleasure. When the factory went bankrupt he made no further effort to find work: by then the agony had abated to a dull needle that was always embedded into his being.

Occasionally he drank, but never in the shack. He would walk into the hills up a rough track that followed the creek to its origin, a fecund highland swamp. Only there, safe in the mud that was impenetrable to any vehicle and barely navigable on foot, did he drink - heavily, with desperation, to oblivion.

He studied books and films from the new Russia as if they were intelligence reports, and what he learned infuriated him, ruining his demeanour for days on end. He often thought of suicide but never quite summoned enough enthusiasm to perform the necessary actions.

He got to the point where nothing was left of himself apart from the rhythmic grind of bodily functions: a defunct life, ambitions and goals now reduced to bitter memories. It appeared as if he was born, hurt, driven to inhuman lengths and hurt again - and all he had to show for those titanic efforts was a sunrise over nothing.

There came a day when he awoke and realized that the fear ruled him no longer. He ceased to care that they may find and kill him - even that was more preferable than his current state.

There was no planning, as such. His subconscious had already determined what to do once he summoned the courage. The finer details came to him without deliberate thought.

Success was unlikely - but if he died, that way he would not die for nothing. He initiated his plan and waited for events to unfold.

He lowered both hands on the railing of the veranda and let out a long breath. According to his watch, eighteen days had passed since he sent the letter, with nothing happening in response. His fists balled with frustration and anxiety: the state of hibernation was over. He gambled all by revealing his existence to a dangerous, unpredictable figure; one part of him panicked, another knew that there was no other way than to proceed.

He did not disclose his precise location, but there were no illusions about ASIO. No one really knew how many of its officers were bought by the KGB in the heyday of the Cold War, but it leaked like a sieve. Even the suspected Soviet mole was allowed to retire with his pension, hated but untouched.

In Russia such retirement would consist of a lengthy interrogation followed by a perfunctory trial, an inevitable sentence and a bullet in the back of the treasonous head.

He grimaced: it was incomprehensible how the West ever prevailed, even temporarily. Armed with its age-old recipes, the Russian state stood for more than a millennium. Its past enemies had long crumbled into history's dust, and it went from strength to strength despite occasional setbacks.

So it was and so it will be, he told the alien purple sun - and if all goes well, his effort will soon contribute to a mighty resurgence of that greatness.

###

Tyres squealed as the ageing Volga followed a convoy of gleaming luxury vehicles around sharp corners, turning into Manezh Square. Once a sacred part of old Moscow, it was now a chaotic clash of stately old buildings and modern office towers, whose occupants looked down on the proletariat through panes of expensive Finnish glass.

"We will soon ask hard questions, and every one of them will need to be answered," muttered Klimov with hatred. His driver nodded assent, clearly thinking the same thought.

The gleaming black Mercedes pulled over in front of a building whose façade consisted entirely of glass - a shining wall of dark-blue panes. Klimov gestured to the driver, and they squeezed into a narrow parking spot, mounting the curb with the right front wheel. Banked-up traffic flowed past them as they watched a short, balding man in a grey camel-hair coat emerge from the Mercedes. He marched inside the office building gesticulating at his assistant, who struggled to keep up with a large briefcase cradled in his arms.

One of the bodyguards ran ahead to activate the heavy sliding doors and stood at attention as his boss walked past, looking straight ahead. The bodyguard then returned to one of the black Humvees and tapped on the glass. The window slid down, and he was proffered a lit cigarette that he began to puff nervously, leaning back against the bonnet.

Klimov spotted a policeman walking towards them with a hostile expression and tapped the driver on the shoulder. In response the latter extracted identification and held it up to the windscreen. The policeman discerned the sword-and-shield emblem from afar and walked past with no change of expression or pace.

"Cold, hard men, our modern militia," remarked Klimov light-heartedly. The driver shrugged his shoulders with muffled indignation. That gesture conveyed, better than any words, that every day the modern militia came to work to do the impossible - fight crime in a country that was ruled by criminals.

After a lengthy wait they saw the bodyguard run back to the sliding doors. They opened, and his boss marched towards the Mercedes with an imperious, sour expression. The guard ran to the limousine and opened that door as well. He closed it gently as the all-important passenger slid inside, lifting his expensive coat away from dirty snow in the gutter. The Mercedes began to roll less than a second later, and the guard did well to board the Humvee that already took off to follow.

"The lord cruises across his dominion," commented Klimov acidly.

"Dacha," replied his driver with hate. The conceited gangster was clearly intent on his country retreat, having dispensed with business on that sunny Friday morning. They had been following Rustamov for two weeks, studying his movements in preparation for an opportune moment. The surveillance was totally in the open, intimidation being an important plank in the campaign.

Times were changing so very rapidly, mused Klimov. So fast, in fact, that few of the pompous fraudsters and thieves - not to mention kidnappers and murderers - who pilfered their way to wealth in the wake of the Soviet collapse, even realized that their fates were now sealed.

Not that they owed their success to any kind of talent or prescience. By and large, they learned to thieve and cut corners as low-level managers in the clod-footed Soviet bureaucracy. With long experience of being professional scoundrels, they were the first to realize that all property of the former Soviet state was suddenly bereft of owner, new reality being that of "finders-keepers".

But that was as far as their talents could get them in this unprecedented jungle. They feasted very well, vultures astride the sickly corpus of a global power - but now it began to awaken. Klimov was one of many senior FSB officers now assigned to hound the so-called oligarchs using tried and proven KGB tactics. Intimidation, harassment, disorientation - then, if bloodless measures failed, violence:

lightning-fast and repulsively brutal.

They followed the convoy down Kutuzovskii Prospekt and turned into Rublevskoe Shosse, the route long travelled by Soviet viziers escaping the grim portents of Moscow to their country retreats. Rustamov made a grand statement when he bought land at Kuntsevo, a semirural precinct once totally closed to the public. Back then only Politburo members were permitted to relax in its woods away from the eyes of sweaty masses. Nothing, alas, was sacred today - or so it appeared to the unwary.

The Volga barely managed to maintain traction in recent snow - fortunately, massive Humvee tyres mashed a path through fresh powder. Klimov's driver was forced to slow down and lose the convoy out of sight, but that was scarcely important - they knew the destination all too well.

They arrived at the wrought-iron gate some minutes after Rustamov's entourage had passed. An ageing sentry glared at them with consternation, but finally resolved to halt their car with a firm gesture of the gloved hand.

The driver rolled down his window and produced identification. The guard studied it and shrugged with indifference.

"FSB, chicken-brains," rasped the driver. "Open right now, unless you want us to remember what you look like."

"I am not supposed to let anyone in," replied the guard with indifference. "You might be FSB, but he pays my son's medical bills. Remember anything you please."

"I will do you a favour," said Klimov, noting a small lapel badge on the guard's coat. "You being a veteran and all - why don't you just tell them we are here? That way you stay out of it."

The guard's watery blue eyes flashed something that could be mistaken for gratitude. He returned to his booth and spoke into a hand-held radio. Nodding at the reply, he came back to the car.

"They want to talk to you."

"Palashev, Mr Rustamov's secretary," crackled a high voice in the handset. "Who are you and what do you want?"

Klimov took the handset.

"We are here to seize your weapons export license. It was rescinded, effective immediately."

There was a prolonged period of silence. Klimov shrugged and handed the unit back to the guard, who returned to the booth and spoke into the radio urgently.

A few minutes later he shook off his glove

and reached for the control panel. Heavy gates swung open.

FSB-plated Volga took off with utter indignity, fishtailing and spinning tyres in deep snow until the momentum began to carry it down the lane into tall forest. They travelled for a good five minutes before arriving at the centre of Rustamov's estate, where a stone house built in the style of Colorado ski lodges stood under tall pines.

A dark-suited man stood on the porch, smoking a cigar with short, nervous gestures. He stared as Klimov emerged from his car, unhurriedly straightened his heavy coat and strolled towards the house, studying it with an air of apparent contempt.

"We will complain," said Palashev with no preamble.

"You will, without doubt," answered Klimov sturdily.

"This is entirely without foundation," continued the man.

"Now, that depends on the width of your perspective," replied Klimov lightly. "As of the last six months, it may be that you were entirely respectable. But if we go back to 1995, for instance, a firing squad may seem inadequate for what you and your flea-ridden boss had perpetrated."

Palashev's dark eyes flashed at the reference to the Muslim origins of his boss.

"In essence, your demise will flow from a total lack of propriety," explained Klimov at leisure. "Every criminal should know when to leave, something your ilk thoroughly fail to comprehend. After a thief runs in and out of every house in a village and makes off with its prized possessions, he needs to run as fast and as far as his legs will allow. He must not build a mansion on a hill overlooking the people he just robbed. Is that really so hard to grasp?"

"It was all legitimate according to the laws of the day," replied Palashev, tossing his cigar into the snow. "We acted lawfully, and we are not running anywhere."

"That, of course, is up to you," replied Klimov, staring at his opponent with contempt. "But what we do next isn't."

"It is, again, a question of wider perspective," he continued patiently and benignly. "When the Soviet Union collapsed, no one quite knew what to do. Handing over the country to your ilk was not a good idea, but it was the only one that came to mind at the time."

"By and large, the strategy succeeded - complete chaos and total collapse were averted. But now the state sees billionaire criminals as an obstacle to restoration of absolute power. You see, it is not Russia's destiny to be ruled by pickpockets and petty thugs. It must only be ruled by those who stand ready to murder millions. Not by thieves who hijack warehouses but by those who purloin entire nations. It must not be any other way. Simply put, it can't be any other way, if we want to move forward."

"Once it begins, we will have all of you rounded up in two weeks. We have facilities to process tens of thousands. You will be swallowed up, and it won't be possible to find your bones amongst those deposited by my predecessors."

Palashev stared at him with horror and a rising sense of urgency.

"The permafrost is melting all over Siberia," continued Klimov dreamily. "Global warming, fuck it. There are many places where rivers erode banks and expose entire cliffs made of bones. Dry bones. Millions of bones. Nameless bones. Bones like ones holding up your expensive suit right now. When the time comes, you may well find yourself digging your own grave, still dressed in the ragged remains of that suit. Now I want to see your boss."

The man nodded and extended his hand, urging Klimov to wait on the porch. He ran inside, not bothering to shut the fine timber door. Klimov smiled with contentment and made a move to follow, but stopped dead in his tracks.

The ring tone of his phone indicated that the call came from much higher than he dared to imagine. He ran down the list of his recent movements, trying to anticipate a possible reprimand and to engineer excuses, but nothing came to mind. He was reasonably certain that Rustamov's intimidation had nothing to do with the call, as that would have come through his immediate superior. No, he concluded, fingers wrestling with the buttons of the heavy coat, this was something else.

He flipped open the phone and stepped away from the house. Palashev came out, but Klimov stopped him at the threshold with a powerful gesture of the other hand.

"Klimov."

"Comrade Lieutenant-Colonel, you will return to headquarters immediately," uttered an officious male voice he did not recognize.

"Do I have an hour to complete a delicate stage of my present assignment?"

"No, leave immediately. You will be met by Captain Pogrebiev on arrival. Brief him on your progress verbally and hand the operation over to him. He will instruct you as to further movements."

"Understood," Klimov waited for the caller to hang up and began to walk towards the car.

"Your brotherhood gets a short reprieve," he told the startled Palashev, replacing the cell phone in his inner pocket. "I have to do something important, and my subordinate will complete this assignment. My final advice is to start looking at real estate in Costa del Sol - personally, I can't understand why you hesitate. The choice is between moving to Spain with all that you had stolen and riding to Kolyma in a freezing cattle truck, to spend the remaining months of your life wearing clothes in which you were arrested. No, I can't understand you at all."

Without awaiting a reply Klimov boarded the Volga, already reversed and waiting, engine running. Leaving the driver to struggle with fresh snow, Klimov closed his eyes and forced himself to review all possible reasons why he would be suddenly pulled away from a successful operation. Whatever he may be accused of, his immediate response will determine the outcome. This was nothing new.

They sped through Moscow and turned into the infamous gates of Lubianka, the FSB headquarters, within fifty minutes of receiving the call. Pogrebiev was waiting for them in the car park, hastily crushing a cigarette with his heel as they rolled to a stop.

The briefing took an additional five minutes,

followed by a rapid walk towards one of the lifts. Pogrebiev pressed the lift button himself, stated the destination and walked away.

Klimov allowed himself a sharp intake of breath - he was summoned by General Lebedev, no less than head of Second Directorate, the foreign operations arm of the FSB. He focussed on his foreign assignments, but that line of thought was clearly unproductive - they were very dated and relatively routine operations. As the lift reached its destination, Klimov was none the wiser about the possible reason for his sudden recall.

The general's secretary waved him through the outer office without looking up - not the best of portents. Klimov pushed open the heavy doors, and they shut behind him silently and firmly. He approached the massive desk and stood at attention on a seemingly priceless Persian carpet.

Lebedev was an elderly man once possessed of thin, craggy features, now blurred by a lifetime of titanic intake of liquor. His steel-grey hair was cropped very short, and his scalp glistened with disconcerting moisture.

The general sat very still, intently listening to whatever was said to him on the phone. He made occasional notes with his right hand, and he appeared to underline most of these notes afterwards. The silver nib of the fountain pen dashed across the paper, and Klimov noted that the bottom edge of the writing pad appeared to be slightly damp, as if the general's hands sweated in profusion.

After a short time Lebedev looked up and examined Klimov with an intent and hostile stare. There was nothing comradely about his gaze, and Klimov noted that he was not invited to sit down.

"Very well," said the general into the phone after some time. "Anyway, he is here now."

Klimov again ran down the list of his foreign assignments, but nothing controversial came to mind. He went back further - but even thinking back to the start of his career, he could not come up with a likely reason for the summons.

The general hung up without saying another word and stared at his notes. The silver pen danced over the sheet, drawing lines that linked underlined words. Then he looked up and studied Klimov, as if doubting his manhood.

"You operated in Australia at the start of your career," he said accusingly.

"Correct, Comrade General."

"For almost ten years."

"Also correct, Comrade General. Nine years and three months."

"Sit down. This is going to be a long conversation."

Klimov went to the indicated chair, breathing out a sigh of invisible relief. It was now certain that he was being briefed about some unexpected emergency, rather than reprimanded for a personal failure.

"A few weeks ago Pertzov's headquarters in the Caucasus received this," the general passed across what appeared to be a photograph of a short document written in a flowing, old-fashioned long hand. "You have five minutes to appraise it."

As the general returned to his notes, Klimov studied the letter until he memorized it. He thought for a while with eyes tightly closed, then opened them and returned the letter to the desk. Lebedev looked up immediately.

"Well?"

"If true, Comrade General, that is a serious development."

"Serious?" The general allowed himself a short laugh. "Where do they get pansy boys like you - we are on the brink of a catastrophe! As if that lunatic wasn't terrifying enough - Klimov, the elections are eight months away, and he is strutting all over the Caucasus, being photographed with his boot resting on dead bodies, promising the return of a proud empire - and now this? Why, the only thing that stops him from becoming our next boss is his body count. That is his only political baggage so far. Imagine if he actually broke the Chechens without losing another soldier."

"Is that technical appraisal credible?"

"Regrettably so. It took forever to access the old archives and to hunt down surviving witnesses. Yes, it fucking well works. They sneaked it into action in Afghanistan, and the result was spectacular. They wanted to implement it more widely, but calmer heads prevailed - heaven help us if anyone in the West figured it out. The bottom line is, yes, it works like a Swiss clock. Other questions?"

"Why me, Comrade General?"

"Why you? Klimov, it's your old stomping ground. It wasn't possible to photograph the envelope, but it has been sighted. That shithead hid in Australia and posted this letter from Canberra."

"Any reason why he went there?"

"Distance, most likely. He probably thought that Americans couldn't protect him on their turf - quite right, too. He went for a more unlikely destination, not realizing the extent of our operations in Australia. The references in the letter suggest that he has no access to anything other than lay media. Western journalists are generally hostile to Pertzov - 'Dark General', 'Cossack menace', 'Russia's Pinochet, at last'. That cur must have drawn the right conclusions."

"It seems so, Comrade General."

"Naturally. Get your underfed arse on the plane - you are the new cultural attache," the general permitted himself an ironic smile. "Our old one has decided to retire for family reasons. That's how much I need you there."

"Understood, Comrade General."

"You will be met by someone from the embassy and received in the usual lace pantie manner. The rest of your team will be inserted covertly."

"Understood, Comrade General."

"Your top priority is elimination of the subject. The secondary priority is to preserve secrecy. That is all."

"Understood, Comrade General. How much time do I have?"

"That's the other terrifying thing - we don't know. According to my source, Pertzov hasn't made any moves from his end - but could do so any second. We don't know, Klimov, we just do not know. Move as fast as you can, and I will try to warn you if Pertzov acts before you are in position."

"Understood, Comrade General."

"Listen, Klimov - you are not a good man for this job. I just don't have anyone else with sufficient local knowledge. If you bugger this up, there will be many consequences, especially if Pertzov succeeds."

"The latter is not an option for our country, Comrade General."

For the first time something of an approval softened the general's haggard features.

"No, it is not. But listen, Klimov. If that happens, don't come back, whatever you do."

"I will consider your advice with great care, Comrade General."

"Great care, indeed," Lebedev's eyes flashed glacial contempt. "If that happens, your life isn't worth a cigarette butt, understand? Do you have a family?"

"Only my wife, Comrade General. No children."

"In that case, she has to go with you. We shouldn't disrupt your cover - that will be put down as the official reason."

"Thank you, Comrade General."

"Don't thank me. As an experienced officer, you will fear the consequences of failure, and I can't afford to have your concentration disrupted in that manner. You have a single day to look through the archives and assemble suitable materials from here. They have digitized the records in Canberra so you can access everything once you arrive. Most embassy materials are sadly out of date, and many of the power players in Australia are not known to the current operatives, such as they are."

Klimov responded by merely allowing his eyebrows to rise.

"Yes, disgusting," said Lebedev. "But things have not been what they should be for years. Australia's been on the backburner - we don't have much going there apart from a few commercial targets. As a sad result, we are caught with our pants down, and you are my saviour."

Klimov nodded politely.

"Which is terrifies me as I am sure it terrifies you. Don't answer - just get on with it."

Klimov took one of the pool cars and made his way through grim afternoon traffic in fading light. By the time he parked his car in the underground garage beneath his apartment, it was nearly dark.

He locked the car with the greatest of care, for these were not the times when a black vehicle with KGB plates could be left on a busy street unattended, windows wide open. He retrieved a large shopping bag from the boot and lugged it to the lift, pressing the button to the top floor. There were a few perks left in the job.

He pressed the modest bell and waited, but nothing happened. Frowning, he opened the door with his key and stepped into the dark anteroom.

A few minutes later his wife emerged from the bedroom. Raisa was a short, thin woman with a mane of ruffled black hair and piercing blue eyes. She was dressed in a rumpled dressing gown, and her eyes were red and puffy with recent tears.

Klimov put his arms around her and held on without words. He needed none to gather that his brother-in-law had not survived his recent heart attack. The news was not unexpected - the man had a vile family history and chose to remain a chain smoker.

Raisa took expensive pills to keep down her sky-high cholesterol levels, but they were making very little difference - her tears were in large part for her own, impending fate. Klimov felt a tightening in the throat - that was something he forbade himself to dwell on. Otherwise life became dangerously worthless for one in command of so many powers and in possession of so many resentments.

He ran a hand down her long hair and loosened the embrace to kiss her tear-stained cheek.

"I too have bad news," he told her gently.

She merely stared, her mouth forming into a determined line. These days bad news came in packs and without warning. One had to be ready to deal with each problem and mop up its consequences as fast as possible - the alternative was to risk defending one's survival on multiple fronts.

"They are sending us back to Australia," he continued.

She closed her eyes to stifle the angry look she was didn't want him to see.

"Vampires," was all she allowed herself in reply. "They won't be satisfied until they suck you dry."

He shrugged his shoulders in a mute acceptance of her statement.

"Call them," she pleaded. "Family circumstances count, surely."

"Not this time," he shook his head sadly. "This one is a real nightmare."

She studied him with alarm. "Dangerous?"

"Don't worry," he smiled with honest reassurance. "A crisis I need to manage, but no - not dangerous to me personally."

"But the funeral is next week," she told him, sobbing. "Marik has to fly in from fucking Los Angeles."

"I know," he stroked her hair. "But this assignment cannot be delayed for anything. It is genuinely important, Raisa."

"Aren't they all," she waved her hand dismissively. "We are important too. We really need to be here now."

"I know," he kissed again, feeling her respond with a little more warmth. "But Raisa, my love, I did not invent this problem."

He felt her nod in a resigned understanding and lean against him.

"When?"

"Now. Well, tomorrow afternoon."

She backed out of his embrace and stared at him with some surprise.

"Must be important, all right. What's the matter - can't Ludenko find his underpants?"

"That's right," smiled Klimov, assuming an officious tone. "The ambassador of the Russian Federation is forced to attend diplomatic circuit parties without a stitch below his waist. It is indeed a national emergency, not to mention a sickening sight."

They both smiled through their pain. Ludenko was an unforgettable oaf - a former KGB thug with no class or finesse. He was tossed this once-important post in the aftermath of the Cold War, as chess pieces of a global struggle were swept off the board by history's uncaring hand.

Australia was once a vital outpost of American power in the Southern Hemisphere, one of the few reliable places south of the equator where one could drink water from the tap and rely on solid support in the struggle against Communist hordes. Saved from Japanese invasion by an American fleet during the last global conflict, Australia was a fervent and sharp-toothed ally of United States during the Cold War, its armed forces and intelligence services proving a worthy adversary to the Soviet pawns, who played out many gambits in the neighbourhood.

Soviet forces worked hard to neutralize that American outpost, developing one of its largest networks outside Europe to subvert it. Thousands of hours and millions of dollars were invested in the Australian Left, coaching antipodean Comrades to dominate the unions, academia and the press - not to mention the formidable Australian Labor Party, which soon became little more than a KGB franchise on the South Seas.

The headquarters from which these mighty labours were coordinated was a complex of ugly buildings in an inner suburb of Canberra: a depressing assembly of dirty cream brick, surrounded a tall, sturdy fence of barbed wire. The roof of every building bristled with a veritable forest of UHF aerials, for effortless communication with Moscow that bypassed the local telephone system.

There is something of a tradition in the Canberra diplomatic circuit - each nation does its best to build an embassy whose architecture reflects something of national character. Klimov didn't know whether the Second Directorate exercised a rare urge for humour or whether it happened by mere coincidence - but the Soviet Embassy did indeed resemble a prison.

The citizens of the Soviet Union thought of their country as a prison-at-large; when a man is actually jailed, he is merely restricted in the choice of exercise yards and fellow inmates.

Raisa dreaded returning to that fenced

compound, from which her husband ranged all over Australia to bribe, blackmail and coach his clients: failures, malcontents, perverts and rejects, meticulously cultivated by Soviet agents to do chores and to stand ready to do the Soviet bidding, should their country ever face USSR in real conflict.

She that such work tended to be monotonous. The most tedious were genuine believers in leftist causes, to whom Klimov and his colleagues had to justify proposed misdeeds. The easiest were equally genuine criminals, who wanted money and favours. Most useful were the dead-eyed cynics who used leftist slogans to climb power structures in academia, unions and bureaucracy. Their ultimate prize was real power, for which leftists parliamentarians had to wrestle with oafish conservatives.

A few promising operators were invited to Soviet Union for an intensive course in Realpolitik, KGB-style. By day they were taught how to turn electoral systems of their native countries to their advantage, and by night they were feted with vices of their choice, their decadence carefully recorded by hidden cameras for posterity.

Whilst Soviet agents ranged the vast expanses of Australia, attending to this far-flung interest of their empire, their wives were held hostage in the abysmal embassy compound. In the old days defection offered certain material possibilities, and those who were allowed to bring their families were given no opportunity for coordinated escape. One family member always had to remain behind the tall barbed wire as the other braved the temptations of capitalist excess, for in Australia such temptations were aplenty.

These days, hoped Raisa, things would be a little more relaxed. Russia was also replete with mansions, limousines and supermarkets. Jeans, rock music and fresh food were no longer shimmering dreams of bedraggled citizens; in fact, Russia offered far more opportunities for the likes of Klimov to get rich. Raisa had no grand shopping habits, but walking to the nearby cafe district without a minder would at least take the edge off waiting for her husband's return from his serpentine duties. She was pleased to return to Australia at the end of summer, when the savage sun lost its vicious bite and merely warmed ageing bones. And this time, who knows, she could be allowed to do a little travel. After nine years of living in Australia she could name the days spent outside the embassy compound.

She sighed her acceptance, broke Klimov's embrace and made for the phone. The conversation with her family was likely to be unpleasant in the extreme.

That sun was almost at the city line, yet it still

burned, even in late March. The last rain a distant, pleasant memory, Sydney's shoreline sweltered and decomposed in the heat. The bay offered no refuge, its shallow waters broiling like a giant, filthy spa, whose evaporation filled the city with industrial-grade humidity - nothing was left unscathed.

Ianni Papadopoulos sighed and wiped his forehead with the short-sleeved arm, his well-toned muscles rippling under brown skin. He was born and bred in this town, but he found its new climate uninhabitable. Each movement left him soaked in sweat, and by late morning his Customs uniform stank, no matter what chemicals he ladled into his armpits.

Ianni remembered that stink all too well from his childhood - father reeked like that all year round. His shirts were washed precisely once a week, on the account of not wanting to wear them out. Dad was handsome enough, a peasant from Crete who wore his fingers to the bone in his well-patronized café, but pride changed to dismay whenever Ianni came too close. It was a severe embarrassment before his classmates, Anglo kids who always smelled of laundry detergent even when they spent the day in the summer sun. Ianni swore he would never smell like that when he grew up.

Yet there was nowhere to hide on the waterfront. Ianni suffered the port in full, with its filthy ships and merciless sun. Stale diesel, rotten fish and rust lurked everywhere, poised to turn his smart, figure-hugging overalls into a stinking, unbearable rags. Ianni was gay to his well-toned core: the sight and smell of his body turned his stomach by midday. Alas, he needed the money, which kept his mother in a tidy, odourless nursing home. Otherwise he would have been back in the chilled comfort of the airport before you could say "fabric softener".

Ianni wiped his sleeve for the fourth time since walking up the ramp onto the deck of "Volodimir", a rusting hulk eternally cursed with other stenches - leaking toilets and stale marine diesel. That complex aroma enveloped the deck, made tenfold worse by the sun.

The first mate spread out an array of worn passports on a lifebuoy container and gestured to Ianni without enthusiasm. Presumed owners of these documents milled around the deck, the aura of cheap tobacco competing with aforementioned odours for the honour of parting Ianni with the remains of his lunch. He wrinkled his nose in disgust and proceeded to study the documents.

They were a motley lot, he noted without enthusiasm, but no different to any Eastern European crew. Lean bodies, faces touched with cheap booze, shabby clothes and rickety footwear. Their documents were equally fatiguing - lengthy, unpronounceable surnames, a profusion of given names, blurred stamps from a myriad of foreign ports and dubious watermarks which he never had the courage to study with care. He stamped each passport after as thorough a perusal as circumstances allowed, then restored the pile to the lifebuoy container with a tired welcoming gesture.

The first mate managed an equally enthusiastic smile of thanks.

Ianni walked back down the ramp, wiping his forehead. He looked forward to late evening, when he hoped to float in the swimming pool inside his apartment complex with a good book. With any luck the noisy twins from the bottom floor would bring handsome boyfriends; he could steal looks at young men and tantalize himself with glimpses of their arousal inside skimpy swimwear. The twins were busy girls, he sighed wistfully.

Had Ianni overstayed his welcome he would have witnessed something of a transformation. The smells and the clothes of those on board did not become any less shabby, but body language changed completely, as soon as the clang of his steps on the rusting ramp receded into the thickening dusk.

The first mate who was long slouched against the rail straightened, flipped his cigarette overboard and issued a string of rapid orders. Four members of the crew ran below-decks and returned less than ten minutes later.

They were freshly showered and dressed in the uniform of the modern backpacker - loose khaki pants with numerous pockets, designer T-shirts and sporting sunglasses. They were clad in expensive walking boots and carried large backpacks.

As the sun slid behind the skyscrapers, the pretend backpackers made their way down the ramp and marched towards the gates of the port. They carried their large packs as if they were weightless, their backs as straight as arrows. Even in the darkness spreading over the city no observer would fail to identify them as a military unit, marching as they were in step, albeit in loose formation, towards the bus station.

Once formed, some habits are very hard to conceal.

###

Klimov woke up in gross discomfort. According to the screen in front of his seat they were over the Timor Sea - not yet the end of the interminably long journey, he thought, but the beginning of the end nevertheless. A residue of discomfort from Bangkok's stagnant humidity still coated his skin with sticky sweat, reminding him what the climate of these parts was all about. It was a hard thing, even for his still-fit body, to go from Russian winter to the steam bath of the tropics.

The aforementioned body was stiff with restless sleep of the past six hours and his arm, which supported Raisa's head, was numb from the elbow down. She slept comfortably enough, and Klimov did not dare move. Every now and again he wriggled the fingers experimentally, wincing from the tingling in the wrist - it just had to be.

Klimov studied his mental state from the bottom up. At the bottom was his physical discomfort right now - a trifle to be ignored.

Slighter higher was the concern about the mission. But during the long journey Klimov refused the temptations of alcohol and scorned the movie featuring round thighs and diamond-bright smiles. Some excellent ideas came to him as he watched plastic American teenagers wrestle with their hormones, minus sound. Having plotted the likely events, he was overly worried about the mission.

He was not even that frightened by the possibility of failure. That would rankle honour, but his relatives were well cared-for. His parents' longevity was not a consideration - alcohol soaked their dreary existence in a small town on the banks of the Volga, and that would see to a short old age. They care little for luxuries, to which they were entitled as befitted their son's rank.

Klimov's sister had married a stolid, older man who worked as a shipping inspector on the great river. The bribes he diligently collected over his lifetime would see to a comfortable retirement. There were no children.

He then confronted his greatest anxiety, one that sprayed ice deep into the pit of his stomach. That sensation was new to Klimov; there had been plenty of occasions when his life expectancy was measurable in minutes, but he was a trained combat soldier. It was his destiny to risk his life from the day he crawled into the world.

But then he looked down at the mane of dark hair that rested on his shoulder, inhaling the aroma of sweat and perfume, studying the grey roots emerging from her scalp.

Raisa shifted slightly in response to his body tightening with the sense of danger. She sighed in her sleep and nestled her head further down, her chin coming to rest against his rib cage. Klimov felt a tear slide down his cheek.

His worst suspicion was confirmed less than six hours ago, in Bangkok's vile airport. His trained eyes had no difficulty picking the unhealthy pallor in her face, and when she suddenly rushed to the toilet, he knew. She emerged ten minutes later with a slightly glazed look in her eyes and sat down limply.

In her haste she forgot to hide the spray bottle that protruded from the pocket of her travel jacket. As Raisa tried to focus on the menu, Klimov could see it clearly. A tiny harbinger of death, that clear plastic bottle with red fluid - now just two-thirds full. Klimov knew that container from raucous evenings with his late brother-in-law, who never parted with the same bottle. Nitroglycerine spray opened the vessels supplying the heart, to relieve attacks of pain that occurred whenever the heart ran out of blood.

"Think, fuck it," ordered Klimov harshly. "You are an operative, not a wet rag. New situation means new opportunities."

And so it did: Australia had excellent doctors. Klimov saw plenty of proof in his time, as Soviet embassy provided the local medical system with an unending stream of challenges. There were neglected cancers, drunken car accidents, the odd obstetric emergency and, last but not least, a lot of heart disease. He never saw the system falter - everyone who went into the local hospital near-dead came out alive and stable.

In less than three hours they would land in Darwin - best to wait until they make the remainder of the trip to Canberra. If he raises concerns, the airline may insist on local hospitalization, and that may be less than ideal. No, he would let Raisa sleep and ensure that she makes the trip with the minimum of disturbance. As soon as they disembark in Darwin, he could call the embassy lackeys. Raisa could see a doctor right away, before even going to the embassy - the trustworthy professional would bring the problem under control. Calm down, soldier. Do your job and let others do theirs.

Klimov shifted slightly and rested his unshaven cheek on Raisa's head.

###

The remainder of Klimov's team had the most tiring journey.

A ship carrying a consignment of Belarus tractors laboured through the Pacific. It too was destined for Sydney, but not all of its cargo was suitable for inspection. Regrettably, machine pistols and grenades are strictly prohibited imports. Their thin disguise in various items of camping gear would satisfy an incurious traffic constable, but there was no hope whatsoever of fooling an inspection in a commercial port.

Even worse, the owners did not have time to learn how to impersonate tourists, and the penalty for this shortcoming was covert insertion. Such cloak-and-dagger acts are usually frowned upon by modern cloak-and-dagger types; too many things go wrong with such stunts.

Australia, however, posed a problem. There were plenty of illegal guns, but most were of petty criminal variety - semi-automatic pistols totally unsuitable for covert action, the rest mainly hunting rifles, their illegally large calibre of little use to a professional. The importance of the mission precluded the use of such implements. If the team was caught with military weapons and arrested, so be it - even at short notice, there were plenty more where they came from.

The dive party was assembled on the stern of the freighter and lowered to the water on a lifeboat platform. The engines stopped on command, the giant ship continuing to glide through the darkness in total silence. Five men hit the water in three second intervals, clutching cargo sleds. Each activated a battery powered scooter, and five tiny dots soon faded on the ship's radar.

They were given thirty seconds to get clear of the leviathan screws. After that massive engines roared back to life, and the ship resumed its course ten miles offshore. The operation caused a minimal dip in speed - observed on satellite, it would not have aroused suspicion.

An hour later five men emerged from the surf in total darkness. On command, they unstrapped the propeller modules and drowned them in the reef, where waves were unlikely to wash them onto shore. Their wetsuits followed, and they pushed their way through phosphorescent surf wearing nothing more than diving knives.

They reassembled on the beach and unpacked on the sand. Running through the Australian bush barefoot and in the dark is not recommended in any weather, and they risked exposure whilst they dressed and repacked just above the incoming tide. Within thirty minutes of making land they were ready to march.

Dawn found them deep in the bush. By the

time they connected with a popular walking trail, they looked dirty, tired and just as ready for a beer as any backpackers who neared the end of the famous five-day trek.

Their dive sleds were buried in the bush near the beach. Sadly, their alloy would never rust or decompose, but thick vegetation made discovery unlikely. One would be very disappointed to find such artefacts in the pristine rainforest, especially if one knew what their presence usually meant.

###

The air smelled pretty bad, even to Pertzov. It always smelled bad in the mountains after a battle - perhaps because of the contrast with fresh local air. He registered odours of soot, diesel, cordite, overflowing latrines and, if one stopped to sample the air carefully, the sickly-sweet reek of day-old corpses.

Such was always the signature of his passage - smoking ruins, corpses and overflowing latrines. He would not have it any other way.

Ruins were well in evidence, the village being razed to the ground. The mosque took a number of direct hits from tank guns on his personal orders, and it was now an untidy smear of bricks and other debris. The men who defended the mosque from the nearby trench were neatly laid out in front of the ruined façade, just in case someone missed the point.

Corpses of women and children who hid inside - whatever was left of them - were carefully collected and trucked away, and those who did that job were plied with industrial quantities of medicinal alcohol. The lieutenant did well to pick younger soldiers, thought Pertzov with approval. It does not do to subject family men to the task of collecting pieces of women and children. Teenagers, on the hand, can wash anything off their minds, provided there is enough vodka to do it.

The dead already began to bloat in the

winter sun. It was almost a pity there was no snow, which showed the blood to maximum effect - on the other hand, the merciful winter allowed Pertzov's force to catch many militants in mid-movement. Not that Pertzov belaboured the distinction - in these mountains, he reasoned, everyone is a sometime combatant.

Even without the contrast of snow, fifty-odd villagers executed by artillery fire made an impressive sight. Their corpses were arranged in a long straight line that maximized the visual impact of numbers. Their weapons, firing pins destroyed, were placed across the chests - or the largest recognizable part of the body. Some corpses were crudely reassembled from mismatched parts, and a neat pile of left-over heads and limbs was erected just in front of the line, as if commanding a squad that was felled and shredded by a wrathful swarm of lead.

Pertzov nodded approval and continued his inspection. Lieutenant Bogrov was a promising young man who understood the new game completely. The Chechens were not going to be broken by intimidation, harassment or retaliation. They respected only overwhelming force, and Pertzov provided that in abundance. The kind the Russian Empire always had on tap - blunt, brutal, inhuman power, delivered with the full might of latest weapons.

It elicited an image - not of a blow delivered by a bullet or a rolling tank, but of a mountain landslide. One could but conclude not to provoke such exhibits.

His adjutant finished an interminable conversation over a UHF radio and ran to Pertzov's side, falling in step behind the commander.

"Comrade General, we have made contact with the blue agent."

For some reason Pertzov thought of Australia as blue. It had something to do with Blue Mountains, a name that once caught his amused eye on the map. "Blue" being the politically correct Russian epithet for "gay", Pertzov's lively sense of humour instantly went into top gear. It was probably wrong anyway, he thought later. Most people think of the Caucasus as brown or grey, yet the predominant colour is lush green.

"What news?"

"He has prepared the package and is ready for extraction, Comrade General."

"Oh," Pertzov frowned in concentration. The time for jokes was over. "Any ideas?"

"We cannot use any of the embassy personnel, Comrade General. Some are sympathetic, but they are under very strict surveillance. Even approaching them has been assessed as unacceptable risk."

"Can't he just travel on his own?"

"Technically, there is no reason why not. He has full freedom of movement. But it would attract attention, and he would not be able to take any materials. He is not trained in covert operations."

"How long will it take him to commence production here?"

"If he smuggles out the templates - six weeks, if we provide all the necessary supplies."

"And we will provide them without fail."

"Of course, Comrade General."

"So how do you propose to get him here?"

"We could meet up with him at a major airport in... his country," the lieutenant instantly lowered his voice. Parabolic microphones worked like a charm in the mountains. "I would propose flying him into Turkey and using a ship to get him to the Abkhazian coast. From there we can pick him up with one of our helicopters."

"No, too risky," Pertzov countered with finality. "A ship, then a tank convoy into our territory, that's the safest way. Once aboard, he can begin to coordinate preparations over a secure link. We cannot afford the slightest misstep in this matter."

"Of course, Comrade General."

A squad of armoured helicopters appeared over the ridge and began a final survey of the valley before landing.

"Back to headquarters," sighed Pertzov sadly.

"Yes, sir," said the adjutant with relief, his eyes sliding over the corpses.

"You are wrong to feel disgust," said Pertzov coldly. "Think this is nasty?"

"Well, it is not a romantic sight," replied the younger man honestly.

"Maybe so, but let me assure you. It is ten times cleaner than what goes on back there," hissed Pertzov, stabbing his finger in the general direction of the capital. "Wait until you are a little more experienced, my young friend. You will learn to appreciate the purity and the honesty of brave men facing each other in combat."

He turned on his heel with contempt and marched towards the clearing as the first of the gunships landed onto wet grass.

"Fucking milksop," he muttered under his breath. "Thank Heaven their time is nearing an end."

###

Raisa fastened her seatbelt and looked around with disapproval. Canberra airport has grown in the years since their departure, its traffic now a continuous, slow trickle. The tacky and expensive shops were not at all an improvement, and the newfangled security measures were as silly as they were intrusive. The homely feel of a backwater airstrip was well and truly gone.

"This is really not necessary," she told Klimov for the third time since they landed. "Let's just go to the compound. I want a nice dinner."

"A nice dinner, on my honour," he promised solemnly. "But doctor first."

The embassy service system still worked like clockwork. A mid-sized silver BMW sped across Canberra, its GPS picking the fastest route with the aid of regular downloads that monitored rush hour traffic.

Klimov looked around the clean emptiness of the suburbs with distaste. Little had changed, he thought - it looks a lot drier, but no apparent change otherwise. These lazy, sated people are so set in their ways.

He read the latest précis about Australia on the way to Bangkok. Things were not as they used to be, that was a solid fact. Climate change had wreaked havoc in a nation that once called itself the breadbasket of the South

Pacific.

The economy still clung to good times on the strength of numerous mineral commodities, but arable land was now at a premium. Urban space was becoming overcrowded, cheap housing swollen with destitute farmers. This dislocation was rapidly deepening social divisions. Pity that didn't happen twenty years ago, thought Klimov. His old team would have had no end of fun in such circumstances.

They pulled into a parking lot of a smaller shopping centre and emerged into the heat. Klimov ushered Raisa inside a modest surgery and sat her down next to the air conditioner, which was labouring to maintain an acceptable temperature. He walked to the receptionist and whispered the surname. She nodded and lowered her hand to the keyboard.

Five minutes later the doctor, markedly overdressed in a white shirt and tie, marched into the waiting room. His round face, brimmed with a scraggy black beard, dissolved in a smile of recognition. He and Klimov had many an interesting conversation in more interesting times.

When the Soviet Union collapsed, the doctor, a Russian-born Jew, was fascinated by the new breed of embassy personnel - young, brought up with far greater leeway and craving to understand their new reality. He also rendered much help to sickly bodies, which the embassy doctor transported in regular shipments.

The subsequent years had not been kind to the healer, learned Klimov in the first few minutes of their reunion. Now divorced and with a small son living on the other side of the continent, he has seen better days. The round face showed evidence of much recent drinking, and the shirt hung on his powerful frame like a gleaming tent. The eyes showed something new, reflected Klimov - the twinkle of self-satisfaction was gone, unmasking the intelligence seasoned with a new understanding of human pain.

But the doctor still transacted his business with old deftness. Within an hour Raisa had her blood sampled, a heart tracing was performed - apparently with no adverse findings - medication was prescribed to bring down her blood pressure, and further action would await the cholesterol results. There is no need for immediate action, the doctor assured. Unlike Russia, Raisa's problem was under control.

Klimov laughed for the first time in many days.

As the silver BMW steered around the afternoon traffic towards the embassy, Klimov used the driver's phone to book a table at the nearby restaurant precinct. His mind, well used to compartmentalizing problems, had drawn a steel barrier between the evening ahead and the task on which he would embark tomorrow. That night he would project relaxation, safety and comfort - until Raisa was deep in her fatigued sleep, there will be no hint of tomorrow in his demeanour.

###

His passport named him as Reinhardt Klein, a native of Bonn. If anyone wanted to know, "Reinhardt" sold outdoor equipment and doubled as a mountain guide whenever finances permitted. With platinum-blond hair, a thin, craggy face and a cruel, chiselled nose, he looked the picture of a Germanic demigod. An SS uniform would complement his features with perfection, and his demeanour was tailored to fit a mental image of an Aryan superman who enjoyed his domain with an unhurried, elastic strength of a steel spring. His posture spoke of a devastating force that overwhelms any possible response, an outcome predetermined before it even came about.

"Reinhardt" sat on the grass next to his pack, enjoying the ice-cold beer in the shade of a large eucalyptus. The backpacker hostel was teeming with guests, and his crew blended in just fine, exchanging smiles with tanned English girls who ogled the sculpted male bodies.

"Reinhardt" made a mental note to take precautions at the swimming pool, where four elite soldiers would stand out far more. One by one, perhaps - and what is the point until the heat dies down anyway? No, the beer will have to do for now.

They were booked to be united with their rented vehicles the next day, which still left plenty of time for the first rendezvous. He felt no anxiety on that score. The mission was clearly of exceptional importance - he could tell that from the number of assigned men alone - yet he did not anticipate danger. One ageing recluse, after all, was unlikely to offer much resistance. "Reinhardt" could take someone like that without help - everything else was obviously mere insurance.

There was more concern about safe extraction. His fiancé discovered herself to be pregnant a few days before the transfer, and "Reinhardt" had to leave before he was able to make arrangements in case he didn't come back.

His subordinates rested in the shade, savouring the beer. As one would expect, they completed the forced march with aplomb. "Rudi" limped ever so slightly - he was wounded in the leg during the previous summer but assured that it didn't hurt.

"Steffi" discovered an annoying manufacturing defect - one of his fancy Italian boots sprang a leak, and he found that the sole cracked in the middle. There was no time to break in a new pair, and "Steffi" filled the crack with epoxy glue from his kit. It would hold for the remainder of the mission, when all their gear was going to be destroyed anyway.

"Reinhardt" upended the bottle and drained the last of the magic fluid. He too was taught to compartmentalize tasks to enjoy the present.

He planned on a long shower, followed by a large steak from the tin-roofed establishment across the road, which filled the air with tantalizing odours. Then a long, well-earned rest - and may it cool down for the night.

What came after that was not something he could not attend to at that point, and therefore it concerned him not at all.

###

Klimov locked the car and looked around. The forest car park was edged with ecologically sound boulders that were torn from their rightful place in the ecosystem. There was nothing else of note - no other vehicles and no recent tracks.

He hefted a small backpack over his shoulders and began to walk uphill. The air was beginning to shimmer with mild heat, and he felt the alcohol of the previous night as the gradient began to steepen.

Half-an-hour later he was standing on top of the hill that overlooked the car park. Some kind soul erected a small wooden bench under a weathered sign that marked the divergent trails. Klimov gratefully sat down and took a few sips from a plastic bottle.

According to his watch, the man he wanted to meet was being impunctual. Klimov sighed - it went with the territory. Indeed, a prompt arrival would be cause for alarm.

Klimov ordered himself to enjoy a rare moment of solitude and peace. It was one of only two tasks of the day, but there was much that required extra thought.

He sat back, wishing he brought cigarettes. Alas, his image of a health-conscious, middle-aged trail runner would be shattered by puffing on his favourite Marlborough. Australian smokers were very much on the back foot, forced out of all public places and hounded as self-destructive weaklings. Klimov sighed - abstinence from smoking was a challenge, not to mention a distraction.

After a lengthy and welcome peace he saw a large sedan of local manufacture pull up next to his BMW in the car park below. A rotund, heavy-set man climbed out and looked around. Klimov wanted to signal but desisted, knowing that he is too far to make sense. The Neanderthal would have to remember the instructions and find his way.

After a little meandering around the car park and perusal of a large billboard map of the reserve, the man turned and began to clamber up the path. Klimov enjoyed the last moments of relaxation, waiting in silence on the bench.

Almost an hour pas the appointed time his companion finally wheezed his way to the hilltop. Klimov studied him keenly and catalogued the signs of unkempt middle age. There were bags under once-fiery green eyes, and the handsome face with a square jaw was now riddled with broken capillaries and puffy with fat.

He tried to dress for the part, in a new-looking tracksuit now soaked with sweat and unzipped to the waist. A bum bag hung awkwardly beneath the bulging stomach, its owner unstrapping the water bottle from its belt as he approached.

Klimov stood politely, ignoring the unfriendly demeanour of the late arrival.

"I can't say that I am glad," said the latter curtly. "I hoped that we've said our farewells."

"My dear comrade, we all thought that," replied Klimov with sincere regret. "But no one knows what life hides from us around the corner."

The rotund man lowered himself on the bench, wiping his forehead with the sleeve. Klimov decided to remain on his feet and upwind.

"How long are you going to haunt me?" asked his companion bitterly.

"Well, it's like this," Klimov decided to apply a little pressure. "We own you. We bought you many years ago, along with the photographs. Remember?"

His companion's hostility deflated like a punctured balloon. The man nodded sullenly.

"So we will come back and make use of you as often as devil takes us," smiled Klimov coldly. "But you can take solace in two things."

"What might they be?"

"We don't want to compromise you,"

explained Klimov. "We paid good money, and we like to take care of our assets. That's one."

The man nodded.

"Two, it is to our advantage to see you climb as high as possible. That should be obvious."

The rotund man nodded, drained the last of his water bottle and stared at Klimov expectantly.

"And what do you want this time?"

"Something you can manage quite easily. We want a strike."

"Is that all!"

"No, not quite all," Klimov thrust forward his hand and began to close fingers to underscore his requirements. "One, we want something important to stop working. Two, it has to be inconvenient to the public. Three, it has to be federal, not state. Four, the dispute has to be stale-mated and remain like that for a few weeks."

"Fat chance."

"Why do you say that, comrade?"

"You really think I can do that nowadays?"

"I can't see why not. Should be easier in

some ways - no one expects that sort of trouble any more, and it should hit pretty hard."

"Well, for one thing, the laws are different."

"Perhaps, but no law can ban a legitimate protest action. That will never come to pass in this fair land."

"I would have to have a good look around and get back to you."

Klimov smiled and shook a long finger in admonishment.

"It needs to happen next week."

The rotund man burst to his feet, his face red with anger.

"That's just fucking blatant!" he shouted. "We can't do things like that any more, you hear?"

Klimov shrugged his shoulders in a gesture of indifference. He bent down to his backpack and unfolded the top flap, extracting a rigid vinyl folder from its innards. He unzipped the contents of the folder and passed over a large black-and-white print.

"You were quite a handsome chap before you took to the bottle," he remarked, stabbing his finger into the photograph.

The rotund man wiped his forehead with a

broad, hesitant gesture and sighed. He lowered his bulk on the bench, staring at the photograph with hatred.

"Yes, that lady is decidedly under-age," said Klimov regretfully. "I am no expert, but you can tell by the shape of the nipples, I am told, that she has not reached puberty. Even though her face looks so knowing... Funny how life can turn."

There was no reply. Klimov reached over and gently retrieved the photograph, stowing it away inside the folder.

"Then again," he reminded with an ironic smile. "If you weren't caught so badly, you would not have come to us for help, would you?"

The man stared at him without a reply. He looked a little too angry for Klimov's liking, but it was a bad time to back off.

"And had you not come to us, you would have remained what you were back then - a big, shambling fool with a weakness for young girls. You know, I don't think you would have done quite as well without us."

"What do you want, precisely?" his companion was now a little less flushed, the organizer taking over from the blackmail victim.

"A big outage with no apparent hope of

resolution," said Klimov. "I am thinking air traffic control, waterfront, postal service. Teachers would be perfect, but it has to be federal."

"You are up to something big, aren't you?"

"You should know better than to ask, but no. On this occasion my interest in your country is very circumscribed. After I get what I need, I go home. For the record, I don't miss this place at all."

"Well, it's mutual," the rotund man told him hatefully. "Anyway - waterfront is the most likely contender. There is always trouble there."

"That will do fine," agreed Klimov. "Not a day-to-day inconvenience to the general public, but stevedores sure know how to make a bit of noise, so it should be quite a thorn in the public eye."

"Hugely damaging economically," said the rotund man. "People are pretty mindful of that these days."

"Splendid. Can it happen very soon?"

"Probably. There were ruffled feathers a few weeks ago - some brothers got caught with their hands in the cargo, as is their habit. Unfortunately, that was a police operation looking for drugs or some fucking thing, and the whole thing went official. The company took a bit of an advantage, if you know what I mean. Sackings, criminal charges, the lot. Didn't go down well, but I leaned on them to drop the matter on the account of the election. Not the kind of publicity the party needs."

"Sounds perfect," said Klimov. "Like sensible men, they simmered down for a few weeks then discussed these unfortunate events when heads have cooled."

"And decided not to let the bloody-minded bosses go unanswered."

"Precisely. Then there must be an impasse, do you understand?"

"Oh, that won't be hard. A bit of a powder keg, the waterfront. Takes a while to put out those fires."

"Do you have waterfront men under sufficient control, or do you need me to assist?"

"No, they've been straining at the leash for a while. Stay away from them - I should manage. Putting them back in the kennel – that might not be so easy."

"There will be time to deal with that."

"Right. Can I go now?"

Klimov smiled and patted him on the shoulder.

"I will go first. You know where to reach me if you need to."

"I hope we don't have to meet again."

"Likewise," smiled Klimov impeccably. "Do you think I like your ilk?"

He got up and put on his backpack.

"I am a decorated soldier of my country, and you betray yours as easily as you breathe. I am a family man, and you are a paedophile."

He stared at the rotund man with contempt.

"Think how much devotion to duty I must have - just to stand next to you without tearing your filthy head from your shoulders."

###

Some hours after Klimov descended the hill and gratefully lit a cigarette in the car, a van with two men left the city.

The moon occasionally glistened through heavy clouds, casting gnarled shadows of trees across the windscreen. They drove in an awkward silence, uncomfortable on the cheap vinyl seats of the van hastily requisitioned from the local trades club, one of the more profitable commercial ventures of their party. The van was left outside a loyal man's house, keys hidden under the rubber mat. They walked to that house from Parliament - just a pair of tired servants of the people, off to their favourite restaurant on foot. Drunk driving has become an unfashionable thing to be caught doing.

A man who hoped to be the next prime minister of a middle-weight power drove the clumsy machine awkwardly, crunching gears and leaning into turns on the winding road. His soft choirboy features were tight with ruthless tension that was never seen in public. Expensive manicured hands that had never known a day's work now sweated on the plastic steering wheel that reeked of tobacco and industrial detergent.

His passenger was a short man with a bland, comfortable appearance that fooled many victims into relaxing in his presence. Barry Stahl, permanent secretary to Reilly, was once a very successful barrister. No one knew why he devoted his razor-sharp, venomous talent to serve a dour politician, but rumours did make their rounds when he took the job. They died quickly - Stahl was a vicious figure, famous for sensitive ears that heard through many a wall, as well as a long memory. The word was that he knew many things about powerful figures, and most things about him were best left unsaid.

At the designated truck stop they pulled off the road and crunched down a gravel track past a deserted toilet block. Arthur Reilly let the van coast into a thick clump of bushes and doused the lights. Some seconds later he cut the ignition and climbed out of the van.

Occasional cars sped past them, and both men winced uncomfortably as lights slid across their faces, plastered all over the media in the months leading up to the election. Neither wanted to be recognised tonight.

As if to add to their discomfort and to make their presence more suspicious, a passing cold front left the air bitterly cold for that time of year. Early fog hung over the road in wisps of cotton wool that floated on a light breeze. The silence of the cold evening was interrupted only by the whine of engines struggling up the hill.

Reilly glanced at the luminous dial of his Swiss watch and studied the sparse vegetation that lined the truck stop, but he saw nothing out of the ordinary. He shivered briefly from the cold and the piercing suspense.

When it came, the sound of footsteps was soft and reassuring. It was a confident business-like gait, neither stealthy nor hurried. A man of medium height and build emerged from the darkness, his eyes sparkling in the moonlight. He strolled up to the van and stopped a few feet away.

Stahl eased his rotund body out of the van and stepped away from the open door. He stared intently at the dark figure, who calmly returned the stare. Reilly took in the powerful neck, the trim, tight torso, the broad, Russian cheeks. The hair was dark, cut short and unfashionably parted. It gave the man a boyish look that belied the concentration - his eyelids were drawn into narrow slits surrounded by a web of wrinkles. He stood in silence, staring at Reilly in expectation of the next move.

Stahl marched up to the newcomer without speaking. He pulled out a device he always carried and held it up in his hand, green lights blinking on the compact display. Stahl ran it along the newcomer's torso and nodded, satisfied that no listening devices were concealed on the man's body.

"Let's talk inside," said Reilly in a neutral tone and slid open the van door.

The visitor casually nodded and climbed inside. Stahl slid home the door and squatted on the seat opposite. The stranger pulled out a small wallet and passed it across.

Stahl took out his cell phone and flipped it open, for Reilly to study the document by the light of the screen. After a brief perusal Reilly turned it towards Stahl, who squinted at the writing, then pursed his lips in sudden concentration.

The front page of the diplomatic passport identified the bearer as Valeriy Mihailovich Klimov, an accredited diplomat of the Russian Federation. The small addendum on the next page identified him as a cultural attache to the Canberra embassy.

Klimov handed them another, smaller document, flipping open the leather cover embossed with an emblem of sword and shield. It showed him in a military uniform with blue flashes on the collar. The text was in Russian.

"Who are you?" asked Reilly in a neutral voice.

"Lieutenant-Colonel Klimov. FSB."

"In that case, this meeting is highly irregular," said Stahl grimly.

"So it is, Mr Stahl, " Klimov retrieved his papers and carefully replaced them. "And risky, for all of us."

"I am intrigued," said Reilly, not untruthfully.

"Gentlemen, I wish to offer you a deal," replied Klimov softly. "It involves the forthcoming election."

They stared at him, slack-jawed. Klimov remained silent, letting the full impact of his statement reach them.

"How?" asked Reilly hoarsely.

Klimov curved his mouth in a gentle smile.

"We believe that a serious strike and other such mishaps may be to your advantage at this point," he told them. "I calculate that your party might gain a great deal from the government's inability to manage such unfortunate events."

Both men were too tense to breathe.

"I see that I have your attention," resumed Klimov. "It is possible to arrange for a series of untoward events to continue until a suitable moment, when Mr Reilly is ready to use his famous negotiating skills to resolve the issue. Such a display of statesmanship, one feels, would present the electorate with an unequivocal contrast to the present leader of your country."

"In return for what?" asked Reilly.

"Information about a defector hidden somewhere on your soil. We need to locate him urgently. As the newly elected Prime Minister, you will have instant access to such information."

"What defector?"

"I regret that I cannot disclose that unless we agree."

"Not a very great return on the risk," said Reilly with disappointment. "At this stage we look pretty bad, but the election is still some days away. That's a long time in politics. What you are offering is too vague and too dangerous."

"Very well," said Klimov and started to leave. He turned around with his hand on the door handle. "Of course, you understand that I can go to the other side with the same offer?"

He could see by the startled expressions that it hadn't occurred to them at all. Klimov smiled.

"Yes, making a hero out of that redneck would really ruin your chances," he mused, hand still resting on the door handle. "But, as you say, a lot can change in a few weeks. Good luck, gentlemen. My natural sympathies lie with you, for old times' sake. But you know what they say in the West: business is business."

"What do want with this defector?" asked Reilly tentatively.

"Drink a toast his long life, no doubt," cut in Stahl quickly. "Much as I am curious, I don't think we should be party to that knowledge even if we do business. Let's not be hasty, Colonel. Tell me, how do you propose to procure such a strike?"

"Barry," said Reilly quietly. "Let's just bid the man good night, go home and hope that the age of such things is long gone."

"Would you excuse us for a minute?" asked Stahl. The Russian nodded and climbed out of a van, closing the door behind him. They watched him walk away and stop next to the bushes.

"You know, it beats the hell out of taking chances," said Stahl. "We don't look that great at the moment, and time is getting short."

"I don't want to get into bed with the FSB, Barry. It's so damn dangerous."

"We are not virgins, Arthur. Look, they must be desperate. Needless to say, nothing like this could have happened without a thorough analysis - I am willing to bet that he has already worked out the safeguards. Old KGB hands don't do anything without exquisite planning - there can be no blowbacks and no publicity. Plus, imagine someone actually accusing us of this. It would be laughed off as paranoid psychosis or a cheap tabloid stunt."

"What about the defector?"

"I think he's as good as dead, one way or the other. If we don't make this deal, the blue bloods will. They are running scared too - the polls are still swinging like a whore's hips, and you know how much is at stake here, Arthur. Whoever wins this election gets the warm seat for a good, long time. Remember what that spiv said last night."

Reilly remembered all too well. The previous year saw an unusual number of expensive mining projects lining up for approval, and political instability was the only thing that could stop the country from challenging Saudi Arabia for the wealth of mining dollars per head of population. If all went well, suggested the analysts, the number of citizens who actually need to exert themselves to maintain the highest living standard on earth could become smaller than ever. A handful of motivated workers could crew ports, gas wells and mines - and the rest of the nation could continue to do nothing on a comfortable salary.

The balance was finer than ever. In agricultural terms, much of the land west of the Divide was done for. There was barely enough water to maintain a few municipal lawns, let alone expanses of once-productive farmland. Many rural postcodes were on the verge of abolition because of depopulation.

Once the nation's meal ticket, agriculture was rapidly on the way to join the manufacturing industry, driven out of existence and buried with token honours three decades before. To this day Reilly could not explain the agenda behind that holocaust. Now there was talk of ceasing maintenance on highways in what was once the wheat belt. Swollen with rural refugees, major city councils were becoming aggressive players in their own right - urban nightmares surviving on expensive desalinated water, they complicated state politics enormously. Tourism was still solid, but nowhere near as easy or profitable as digging up mineral ore and loading it onto bulk carrier ships from Asia.

Three decades of relative prosperity and low taxes failed to stimulate other industry. They had, however, cemented voters in the belief that their fabulously wealthy nation owes them a living, not necessarily in return for effort. Unlike in times gone by, life became very expensive, and the demise of the rural community exacerbated the real estate circus in coastal cities. The price of basic shelter made it hard to survive on an ordinary wage, and the slightest downturn in the economy threatened to dump millions of over-mortgaged voters out of their homes.

The welfare system was bursting at the seams with former farmers - like the redundant factory workers of the previous generation, they were too demoralized to look for other work, many of them gleefully bleeding the government that bled generations of farming families in days gone by. Their persecution was deemed to be too damaging politically, and increasing numbers of climate change victims were draining the public trough.

None of that was news to mining executives, who felt the difference between Saudi Arabia and Australia very acutely. Saudis were ruled by a criminal clan, whose sole task was to maintain comfortable conditions - so long as countless billions poured into Swiss accounts, the population was kept dumb and content. The Saudi royal family was very aware of how its bread was buttered.

In contrast, the fickle democracy of Australia provided the mineral industry with a constant stream of surprises and headaches. There was a swirling rumour about a secret cabal of mining executives, who had committed themselves to put in power whoever keeps bureaucrats, Aborigines and greenies away from their machinery.

"How can Klimov orchestrate strikes?"

"Please, sweetie," Stahl seldom stooped to sarcasm, and this was evidence of rare impatience. "For five decades union bosses went to Moscow, to be fed, plied with drugs and whores, get lessons in politics, and they got suitcases of dollars every Christmas. There is nothing a man like that won't do - and look, many of them still wield real power. The last thing he wants is his picture, in bed with some pretty KGB doll, or a reminder of how much Soviet money he received in some Canberra motel."

Reilly looked unconvinced.

"In any case, it's not our worry how they create the strike," Stahl persisted. "They have to do that before we need to do anything. And if we don't get in - well, we won't be in a position to deliver, will we?"

"That's true," agreed Reilly. They stared at each other inside the dark van, their minds racing through the options.

"But if we get in..." mused Stahl, looking out the window at Klimov, who stood in the moonlight like a man out for an evening stroll, not a care in the world. "If..."

Reilly stared at him with hunger he could not control.

"If we get in, there is nothing that we won't be able to bury," said Stahl slowly and deliberately.

"You are right," Reilly nodded towards Klimov. "Call him back."

Stahl opened the door and motioned Klimov to come in. The Russian climbed inside and came out a few minutes later. An enigmatic smile played on his thin lips, but as he disappeared into the scrub with his cat-like gait, the expression on the moon-lit face changed to overwhelming contempt.

Reilly climbed out and stared after him into the bushes.

"I can't wait to find out what they are up to," he muttered under his breath.

###

Klimov held on to the handle mounted above the passenger door, to stop being bounced against the metal in a most painful manner. The last hour of the trip from Canberra to the South Coast was proving uncomfortable.

"I am sure this haste is unnecessary," he said in a firm tone. "In fact, it may draw unwanted attention."

"Reinhardt" did not react in a perceptible manner, but slowed the large 4WD slightly, and the ride improved. He pretended to concentrate on piloting it through the deep ruts to avoid the acknowledgement which his superior was owed.

Klimov's mouth tightened.

"How long before we get there?" he asked calmly.

Without a reply "Reinhardt" slid the GPS from its anchor at the windshield and passed it across. Klimov did not reach for it.

"Your superior officer has asked you a question," he rasped, staring at the driver. "What is this bazaar?"

"Reinhardt" slowed down and turned to stare back, but Klimov was ready. His hazel eyes were now narrow embrasures in a face tense with anger - mouth a tight, bloodless slit below a flared nose that sported a few bends from his days as a boxer. He allowed his right hand to rest on the clasp of the seat belt, ready to release it in case freedom of movement was suddenly required.

Another second of that silent duel saw "Reinhardt" back down.

"My apologies, Comrade Colonel," he said gruffly. "I was merely trying to return to camp by the arranged time. There is no way to contact them, and they have certain orders in case we don't return on time."

Klimov nodded and took the GPS. "Reinhardt" threw the vehicle into gear as Klimov studied the small screen. The camp location was marked by a golden star in the centre. A blue arrow indicated their position some kilometres away.

"We may be able to radio from this ridge," said Klimov. "Are they listening?"

"Under orders to maintain radio silence, but yes, they are receiving, Comrade Colonel," replied "Reinhardt", now maintaining deferential tone.

When they neared the top of the ridge Klimov lifted the microphone from the CB unit at the dashboard.

"It's on the correct frequency," said "Reinhardt" in anticipation of the question. "We are Bill, they are Hilary."

For the first time in many days Klimov burst out laughing.

"Man, you are behind the times!" he bellowed, slowing the vehicle with a gesture of his hand. "It should most certainly be the other way around."

"Reinhardt" smiled, appreciative of Klimov's effort to dissipate the tension between them.

"Hilary, this is Bill," said Klimov in English. "You probably don't have the wattage to reply, so just listen. We are on top of the ridge and will be arriving in a normal manner, ETA sixty minutes from now. You should have a swim before we arrive."

"They will appreciate that," said "Reinhardt". He selected a gear, passing the top of the ridge more slowly. "Hold on, Comrade Colonel, this is a nasty descent."

He was assuredly right, decided Klimov mere minutes later. The fire track followed the course of what was once a waterfall, now a dry stony staircase running straight down the mountain slope. "Reinhardt" slowed, allowing the vehicle to clamber over rocks with minimal speed at a precarious angle. He kept both feet off the pedals, allowing the engine to brake near-slide. It was clear that a single slip would cause the wheels to lose traction, sending them out of control.

Being an expert of his trade, "Reinhardt" negotiated the worst of the slope without incident, and Klimov was able to wrench his attention away from the track. He stared into the tall bush, taking in the details.

Since his last foray into that country the undergrowth had died back, leaving only taller trees that were able to access enough moisture and sun. These days it only rained a few times a year, he was told, and the vegetation was now quite different.

Klimov never liked the Australian bush. It was far too different from what he called a forest, where one stands at the bottom of a green ocean of massive pines and deciduous trees, redolent in perfume of fecund soil, mushrooms and rotting leaves. Russian forest can be traversed without impediment, for most of the wood is soft and rots away after only a few seasons on ground. The soil is damp underfoot, but one seldom circumnavigates obstacles like fallen trees.

In contrast, Klimov remembered Australian forests as a tangled mess of fallen trees and dense undergrowth, where a few kilometres a day was as much progress as one expected to make.

Now the undergrowth was thinner and looked less impassable from the road.

Nevertheless, he saw for the first time, it too had beauty. The colours of the South Coast are especially stark: the stormy sea is bright green and turns a startling sapphire-blue during calm. Soil ranges from white to crimson red and even deep purple. Trees are another shade of succulent green, and the electric blue of the sky is seldom visited by cloud. Klimov wondered if he could ever live in such a place; as "Reinhardt" brought the vehicle through a stagnant creek that marked the end of the descent, he came to a surprising conclusion that he could.

Once on even ground "Reinhardt" floored the accelerator, and they raced towards the beach. Their progress was interrupted by a fallen tree - Klimov began to reach for his seat belt clasp, but "Reinhardt" held up his palm, motioning for him to remain in place. He approached the tree at a slight angle and pressed a button on the panel to engage the centre differential for more traction.

The engine grunted as the bonnet rose upwards. There was a heavy thud as the chassis slid over the tree, mercilessly driven forward by the rear wheels. It hung over the tree for a few seconds as the engine surged, suddenly freed of its task as all wheels left the ground. Then the bonnet tipped down slowly, and the front wheels caught, dragging the vehicle the rest of the way.

"Very classy," remarked Klimov.

"Reinhardt" nodded. "Land Rover. No one makes them better."

"I am sure the driver's skills are just as decisive," said Klimov.

"A little, Comrade Colonel," replied "Reinhardt" modestly.

"Wouldn't it be easier to drag that tree out of the way?" asked Klimov.

"But we took such trouble to cut it down," explained "Reinhardt". "We didn't want company in our little encampment."

Klimov nodded belated understanding.

The vehicle slowed down as water came into view. Klimov saw the low domes of the tents, pitched under the trees in a rough semicircle. A campfire was constructed on the beach, with large pieces of driftwood serving as seats.

"It's remarkable cold at night," explained "Reinhardt".

A number of men emerged from the ocean stark-naked. They unhurriedly restored their clothing as Klimov emerged from the car, stretching his stiff body. By the time he retrieved his back pack they were assembled in a perfect straight line.

He faced them and drew to attention. They reciprocated in perfect unison, saluting him without command. He returned their salute, and eleven muscular arms dropped down, moving as one.

"At ease, men," he told them. The bodies shifted into a more comfortable posture. "Get something to eat and reassemble here in ten minutes."

They ran in different directions as he looked at the water longingly. Even though there was not a lot of time, even a dip would make him feel better and allow greater concentration, he decided. He threw off his clothes and ran into lukewarm surf, dropping down into lapping waves and letting them take salt and heat from his skin. He remained in the shallows, rubbing his body with sand until quite cleansed.

He restored his clothing, leaving off the boots. The fire was not lit in fear of attracting park rangers, but the food was pleasantly fresh and went down well with cold beer he and "Reinhardt" brought with them in plentiful supply.

"This operation will consist of a number of phases," Klimov told them. "We expect to remain in the country for less than six weeks. The first part is relatively easy, but then it gets much, much harder - you should not underestimate what we are up against."

###

The fire in the rusty oil barrel was not much help against the elements, and Cliff walked the length the picket line to keep warm. The icy breeze coming off the sea brought scattered drizzle, which maximized his discomfort.

They were nearly out of firewood; with five hours of the shift to go, he was beginning to regret this chore. But money under the table was a welcome relief from pressures caused by his pervasive habit. Cliff couldn't go past a racecourse without sharing his wealth.

The other comrades were snoozing in a makeshift shelter, their cheap sleeping bags little use in the night that was headed straight for a cold front. Still, it was better than the alternative - Cliff's better half was a large mound of lard, decorated with prison tattoos and lately neglectful of personal hygiene. Their relationship was cemented by common complicity in certain past activities. In fact, the cement was little more than blackmail.

Cliff, on the other hand, scrubbed up well, his still-powerful frame topped by a head with rugged features. The red hair was a little thinner than he would like, but women were not known for pushing him away with disgust. Alas, breaking faith now could mean that his next date was consummated in jail, and he suffered the relationship with dignity.

At least the picket job was simple. There was

no traffic, no angry contractors and not a whiff of demonic scabs. They might as well have set a picket line in the outback.

As always when Cliff had time to think, his thoughts turned to a toddler with huge green eyes and a mop of Cliff's own red hair. The last time Cliff saw him, the boy was dressed in a ridiculous purple jumpsuit. Cliff was allowed to take him to play in the park, all under the watchful eye of a malodorous dyke from social services. He watched the toddler rampage in the playground and roll in autumn leaves, getting mud all over the jumpsuit. He remembered the cool May sunshine and smiled. It was a happy day.

A week later the boy's mummy disappeared from her government flat. A while later they stopped taking out child support from his dole - her bank account was suddenly closed, and she could not be traced. He turned to his heavy-duty friends with a most honourable of requests, and they even did some asking around for free. But nothing turned up. There was no millionaire husband and no police pursuit, no bodies in the morgue, no overseas flights - nothing. Just wanted a new life, was what the elderly private detective told him with sadness. New identity is not that expensive, and if she used it to leave the country, then he could look for a hundred years.

Cliff was left with the memory of the day in the park. He replayed that memory at frequent intervals, fearful that one day it may fade in his very ordinary brain.

He resumed pacing, feeling his throat tighten with a hurt that never failed to sting. Time had dulled that loss, but only just. Since then there were many women and many contraceptive failures, both accidental and semi-deliberate on his part - but obviously, his shooter was not always loaded with live ammo. If there were any more red-mopped children, he was not informed - and perhaps it was better that way.

He suddenly tensed up and turned towards the road. A pair of headlights crept towards the picket line, and he studied them with resentment. Surely some drunken fuckwit who lost his way – what a place to do it.

His right hand tightened around the metal bar he ostensibly used as a walking staff. Cliff crossed the road and positioned himself on the driver's side of any approaching vehicle, ready to challenge the occupant without standing in his path. He stood a few pickets in his day.

As the headlights came close, Cliff's breath tightened in alarm. It was a company van, all right - and it looked as if it carried a few scabs. He squinted as halogen beams bounced over the rough paving of the wharf, then put out his hand in a forceful gesture for the driver to stop.

The headlights continued to crawl towards him, and Cliff became aware of an incongruence - the note of the vehicle was not the diesel clatter of a standard shipwright's van. Instead, he registered with alarm, it was a low growl of a powerful V8. The tyres were all wrong as well - low-profile jobs on expensive allow wheels.

"Dockers and Shipwrights Union picket!" he bellowed, hoping to awaken his lazy mates in a big hurry. "Do not cross!"

"Urgent delivery," replied the driver, a blond man with sharp features. He was calm, registered Cliff, too calm for what he was doing: running a picket line of the biggest strike in decades, with only a few men in a single vehicle. None of it made any sense, and the quicker others arrived at the scene, the happier Cliff would feel.

"Do not cross," he repeated loudly, his voice trembling a little with anger and fear.

The door on the other side slid open, and Cliff became aware, rather than saw, one of the occupants emerge from the van, moving around it swiftly. There was something seriously wrong, Cliff realized too late. It was the way the man moved - like a hunting animal, shoulders down and head forward. The dark figure made no sound as he surged towards him.

Cliff took a step back and raised the metal staff, but the shadow clad in a black boiler suit ducked the heavy blow, dashing right and then left. A blade flashed in the darkness, and Cliff felt his legs fold beneath him.

He collapsed to the ground as the van spun wheels, reversing down the wharf. It was expertly turned around in a minimum of available space, then the throaty sound of its engine died in the distance.

Cliff heard a rush of voices as merciful fog enveloped and drowned his rising distress. He lay in a pool of blood and smiled, seeing the red-mopped toddler in a purple jumpsuit with a clarity he never saw before. The boy hobbled towards his father and grinned an earnest, empty grin of a happy child. All was finally well.

Cliff smiled back as he died.

###

Collins sat in the rear seat of the car, leaning back against the smelly vinyl with his eyes closed. The vehicle sped down an empty freeway towards the dawn. It was nearing seven, and Collins was awake for four hours.

The driver, a young constable, had turned on the flashing lights but left out the music in deference to his fatigue. He concentrated on maintaining his speed just above the speed limit, the late-model pursuit vehicle absorbing the distance with ease.

Collins resented politics that yanked him out of preparing for retirement and dumped him into this nasty, urgent filth. Especially in the early hours of the morning - he did not sleep well at the best of times. Waking the neighbours to make arrangements to have Penny fed and walked was a major call on their good will, and that was not pleasant either.

Grudgingly, he had to admit that the job was urgent. The situation was explosive - a picket line unionist killed at his post in the middle of the most destructive and controversial strike in living memory. Not Collins' memory, for he was rather long in the tooth - but there were plenty of adults who were born after the last event of that kind.

He could not blame the boss from calling all cavalry. This one had to be solved fast, and there was to be no appearance of sloth. Civilized society had to step in and blow the whistle on the way the strike was playing itself out, and it had to be done before anyone could say that the wretched government had anything to do with it. Election year, no less. Conspiracy city.

When he next opened his eyes, they were speeding through the central business district that was stirring awake in a pollution-laden dawn. The smog actually enhanced the sunrise, thought Collins with amusement. How pretty.

The pursuit car sped down the exit ramp and turned into the port, barely slowing. Collins straightened his tie and ran a hand through what was left of his hair. The day ahead was going to be very long.

###

Collins' distaste for the surroundings was tempered by the widow's tears – which seemed entirely unfaked.

He would have loved to understand what kept a relatively serviceable lad like Cliff in a company of that prison bird - but Collins had long given up trying to understand the foibles of the heart. He was something of an expert on greed, hatred and aggression - but travails of love seldom darkened the door of his office.

He summoned the will to ignore a mixture of stale odours - poorly vented frying, unwashed body, unchanged bed, stale dishes, old dog, plus a few other uncomplimentary smells that he registered with unwelcome clarity, now that he had given up smoking.

The bereaved woman sunk deep into the cheap vinyl sofa, abundant tears streaming down her pasty face. She had an expression of someone whose generally low expectation of life has just been reduced beyond all imagination. Collins was reasonably certain that it was not an act.

"What fucking enemies," she sobbed. "He was as gentle as a lamb."

Collins was aware of a few moments in Cliff's biography that contradicted her description - the court records left no doubt on that score. Nevertheless, the widow was broadly correct - acts of violence were few and far in between. The documented exceptions, for which Cliff spent a few months in jail, appeared to be fuelled by alcohol or unrequited love.

"What about his ex-wife?" asked Collins out of good form. He already checked and knew that the latter disappeared. The disappearance was clearly engineered, judging from hasty sales of property and closure of bank accounts – and on the surface, Cliff seemed very unlikely to have had anything to do with it. The ex was yet to be found, but Collins held little hope of anything useful from that effort.

The woman blew her nose into a soggy tissue and examined its contents by reflex. She looked up at Collins, her pale blue eyes awash with pain.

"Disappeared, the fucking whore," she spat, colour surging to her face. "He was real cut up, Cliffie. Never saw his boy again."

Collins nodded with unfeigned sadness. He checked into that too - no trace of the child either. Maybe that angle was worth another look.

"No contact at all after that?" he repeated for certainty.

"Nah."

"Debts?"

She nodded wistfully.

"Drugs?"

"Nah. Gee-gees."

Collins looked up sharply.

"Know any names?"

"Rocky, Jim Scanlon and Rattie. He never went to no one else."

The young detective from Melbourne was writing furiously. Collins nodded.

###

Pertzov reached forward and selected a large pickled cucumber from the aluminium bowl, looking around with distaste.

His staff were dining in an ancient house - a pile of uneven stones cemented to wooden pillars driven into the side of a steep hill, as were most houses in the Caucasus. The owners were persuaded to reside with neighbours by means of presenting them with a box of AK-47 rounds. Pertzov shifted on a rough wooden bench with distaste - he didn't mind the rough surroundings, but the bedbugs he was likely to battle in the night were another matter.

Which was entirely symbolic of the war, he thought grimly, watching as Bogrov filled a small crystal tumbler with vodka, stopping just short of the brim. It was easy enough to occupy territory and hoist one's flag. But real trouble came later, as the apparent victors were bled in their sleep.

There were a few losses earlier that day, and when Bogrov finished pouring from a large flagon of chilli-flavoured vodka, Pertzov lumbered to his feet, resplendent in his Cossack uniform. He preferred that to fatigues, now that winter had eased. Modelled on traditional Caucasian dress, it reminded the locals that the Russian Cossack is as much a native of the region as themselves - and no less accustomed to warfare in its difficult terrain.

The first drink was to the dead - drunk in total silence without toast, entire glasses tipped down seasoned leathery throats. A short period of silence was observed afterwards, then Pertzov sat back down and glowered at his officers.

"We should have waited for the sun," he admitted. He ordered the attack without adequate helicopter reconnaissance, dense fog covering the valley in the early morning.

His subordinates busied themselves with filling their bowls with food. There was no polite way of acknowledging Pertzov's admission.

"We now need to discuss another matter," rumbled Pertzov. The cucumber sailed into his mouth intact, and he crunched it mightily. "The blue agent."

There was a low murmur at the table.

"What a bunch of old women," roared Pertzov angrily. "Spare me this pathetic sight - are you Cossack officers or used-up whores?"

"Comrade General," said an older man with colonel's epaulettes on his crisp fatigues. "I feel that more consideration of the consequences is required."

"How very diplomatic," replied Pertzov, anger leaving his voice. He reached over and lifted the flagon of vodka to refill the colonel's glass. That was to be taken as a conciliatory gesture.

"Comrade General, I had familiarized myself with the reports from Rebirth Island. That includes the reports of field trials in *Afgan*," the colonel nodded his thanks and clasped a scarred fist around his full glass. "The agent was used in remote valleys with great effect. But the idea was that no one can leave the affected sites and spread the infection in time. When they become infected, it takes too long to walk out - by then the virus does its job, and all targets die before they reach other populations."

Pertzov continued to fill the glasses around the table, expert hand stopping just short of the brim.

"Continue."

"Comrade General, that assumption was entirely reasonable in *Afgan*. But in the lowlands of the Caucasus it is highly likely that an infected subject will reach a large city before succumbing. I am saying that Grozny, Vladikavkaz and Krasnodar may be affected.

Pertzov sat back and looked at the speaker

sharply. His gaze lost focus as he thought.

"So we need a blockade," he said finally. "Well, we can do that. As soon as the first cases begin to emerge, why - it's our duty to isolate the outbreak."

He looked around with a radiant smile.

"Perfect," said Bogrov. "No trucks, no trains, no planes - nothing goes in and out once the epidemic begins."

"That's right," echoed Pertzov happily. "No food, no medical supplies, no evacuees. Maybe the odd mission of mercy - drop a few crates of dehydrated peas and bandages. Seal the fuckers in their valleys, then look for survivors and reward them with more virus drops."

"To our success," he raised the glass towards the centre of the table, to be met by other glasses. Another round was tipped down the throats.

"We need to develop a plan before we get too merry," he said, putting his hand over the glass as Bogrov reached for the vodka flagon. "We are having some difficulty with extraction. Bogrov, explain."

Bogrov let go of the vodka flagon.

"The subject is not much of a field operator,"

he explained apologetically. "Not unfit, but in his fifties and in hiding for most of his adult life."

"How the hell did he defect in the first place?" asked one of the Cossack officers whose helicopter badges sat somewhat incongruously on his lapels. "Didn't he run from Rebirth Island?"

"Yes, he did," said Bogrov, his tone remaining apologetic as if he personally allowed the defection. "There was an outbreak, and things went mad for a while."

Pertzov looked up with interest.

"I didn't know about that," he said curiously. "What happened?"

"A civilian hydrology ship was doing a survey of the Aral Sea. Apparently, it came too close to the island," said Bogrov. "It was immediately detained and escorted to the island. The crew went into isolation, but a few of them and some security personnel developed the disease."

"Which one?" asked the helicopter pilot.

"Same strain of small pox we are discussing," said Bogrov. "It was chosen because the skin lesions appear very late in the illness - in fact, many subjects appear to die first. Makes it even harder to diagnose and formulate an early response."

"Is there a chance that our friend engineered the outbreak?" asked Pertzov.

"I don't think there is any way of knowing that now," replied Bogrov pensively. "What is certain, however, is that he used the incident to disappear. He stole a patrol boat and ran for the mainland."

"So fucking what? Why didn't they shoot him out of the water?"

"Apparently, they could not take off until the infection lockdown was over," replied Bogrov.

"We should handle this man with great care," said Pertzov. "That much is clear. What happened after he got to the shore?"

"That was never quite understood," Bogrov told him. "But he made it all the way across the desert to the Caspian Sea and then to Iran, which was run by Americans back then. We received a report about his presence in their Tehran compound. He must have sold whatever he had, then asked to go into hiding. It is strange that he chose Australia. He must have been unfamiliar with our network in that country."

"Not very reassuring," concluded Pertzov. "He plays dirty and he is capable of sudden and heroic moves. What next?"

"Dirty he may have been, but he lived in isolation since. Possibly not in a safe house all these years, but most likely under supervision, if not under surveillance. He probably has a good supply of cash but would not be allowed to acquire any skills relevant to the present situation."

"In other words, a talented and daring dilettante," summed up Pertzov. "And we need to smuggle him out of a well-sealed country."

"Correct, Comrade General."

Pertzov's gaze turned to a tall man who sat silently at the other end of the table. He wore a camouflage uniform with paratrooper's wings. A thin, hatchet-like face complimented his lean frame. He was dark-haired and deeply tanned, but his short moustache was nearly grey and parted with a long scar that ran the entire length of his left cheek.

"Well, one thing is clear," said Pertzov. "This is a delicate matter, not at all a job for lusty cut-throats like ourselves. We have to defer to Major Leikin at this point: he is ex-GRU and has much experience relevant to our needs."

The officer nodded in reply.

"It should not be difficult," he told them. "But the subject must not do anything by himself. That is not reliable."

Pertzov nodded.

"I have a few men that are suitable for this operation," said Leikin. "At least two of them should be available for immediate insertion. Their job will be to shepherd the subject and to protect him from interception before evacuation can be organized."

"Interception by whom?" asked Pertzov.

"We must assume that his letter has compromised him," replied the major. "At this end or otherwise - we should not go into this now. We should instead assume that Australian authorities will be alerted to a change in his status through observation of his activities."

"Explain."

"If there is a leak from this end, he is as good as gone. We simply have to assume that no such thing has occurred, otherwise it's all for nothing anyway."

Pertzov nodded.

"Continue."

"We will know soon enough if he is still at large," continued the major. "Assuming so, the next danger emanates from his own attempts to prepare for departure - sales of assets, withdrawal of cash from bank accounts and so on. If he is smart, he will remain totally motionless - but we cannot rely on that assumption either."

"How soon can you move your assets?" Pertzov removed his hand from the glass, which Bogrov began to fill instantly.

"With your permission, Comrade General, I will leave this happy gathering and make some calls. The men I want to contact are easiest to reach late at night."

"Permission granted, reluctantly," rumbled Pertzov, raising a full glass. "To your speedy success, Major. Just don't make too many mistakes - we can't afford the time."

"Comrade General," the officer nimbly rose to his feet and drew himself at attention. He snapped a swift salute and gathered his papers into a leather folder.

"It is not my habit to be mistaken."

###

Rattie emerged from the red brick toilet next to the racecourse, shaking water off his hands. At least, thought Collins, one hoped it was water.

He studied the small man who lived up to his name, wearing a drab grey overcoat and a trademark pork pie hat of the same colour. His facial features were clearly the origin of his nom-de-guerre - diminutive cheeks with a long nose that presided over stiff moustache, also mostly grey and mottled from tobacco.

Rattie accompanied Collins towards the car with a professional demeanour. He clearly expected the visit.

Collins opened the rear door and carefully studied the body language as the bookie got inside. Precise, polished actions. Not at all stiff or awkward.

Collins walked around the car as slowly as possible, opened the opposite door and levered his bulk into the rear seat beside Rattie. He left the door open, on the account of a rancid chain smoker smell. The driver remained in his seat, picking his nails with the handcuff key.

"Cliff Saunders," said Collins without a preamble. Rattie nodded.

"Yeah, knew 'im," he replied with a surprisingly velvet voice.

"Midlands?" asked Collins with surprise.

"Bristol, guv," replied Rattie with a joyous smile.

"Been there a few times," said Collins with less than enthusiasm. "Owe you money, poor Cliff?"

"Six-fifty, guv."

Collins sighed. That figure was similar to what Cliff owed other bookies. Even put together, none of them made for an acceptable motive for murder.

"Ever get heavy with him?"

"Must be joking, guv," Rattie waved both hands in a gesture of repelling the statement. "Cliffie was a good boy, see. Always good for it, knew 'e wouldn't be able to come back otherways. Nae need to get 'eavy."

Collins accepted this statement in full – if Rattie lied, he did it far too well to be caught out, and what he said made sense. Being a pessimist, Collins accepted the testimony with equanimity. All facts about the murder pointed away from Cliff's mundane personal affairs and towards the business of unions, strikes and politics.

"Know anything else?"

Rattie shook his head resolutely.

"Kissed me money goodbye," he replied with a hint of sadness. "Ah well, I seyz. Made plenty from poor Cliffie in me day. Nae need to get greedy. But if I get to know something, I'll be beating down yer door, guv. The dick'ed that killed 'im has cost me quid, and I'll be takin' that personally. Know what I mean?"

Collins acknowledged the truth of that statement as well.

"All right then," he replied wearily. "You hear anything, call."

###

Busloads of demonstrators began to arrive early, clogging up the back streets of the central precinct. Formally, the assembly point was a large car park behind the central rail station, but unannounced roadworks made short work of that plan.

A large crowd began to ooze down Burke Street, urged on by union organizers with megaphones. In fact, not much control was required - there was a lot of good-natured banter as the crowd awaited the appointed hour.

On the stroke of ten o'clock someone began to wail 'The International' through the megaphone. The antique melody reverberated between tall office buildings that hemmed in the old rail yard, causing curious office workers to flock to their tinted windows. A few ragged voiced caught the tune, if not words, and the head of a long procession begin to wind their way towards the distant parliament building.

Traffic was hurriedly diverted by police vehicles parked across intersections. Police presence was low key, with only a few officers in fluorescent vests visible here and there. Further back, well away from the crowd, were squads in riot gear. They were visible to the demonstrators, but one had to look hard.

"Reinhardt" marched along gaily, holding one handle of a long, angry placard. He was decked out in soiled blue overalls, whose trousers were draped over combat boots. His very short hair was concealed by a greasy woollen beanie, and he wore wraparound sunglasses, which had some hope of protecting his eyes from flying fragments.

He registered an elevated mood not at all appropriate for what was about to happen. Analyzing, he realized that he was a victim of simple childhood nostalgia. The last time he was in a large, ragged crowd marching with red placards, he was a child in Murmansk, the northern port city where he grew up. It was May Day, he recalled, a festival the Soviet Union took seriously – and back then the Soviet Union was the most dangerous power on earth.

He recalled that the air was colder, with pale sun of the Arctic Circle barely warming the air, and reluctant buds were trying to awaken from the long winter. He walked beside his father, a welder in the submarine pens on a rare day off. It made for a pleasant childhood memory.

"Reinhardt" slipped his hand into the pocket and unsafed his pistol. They were almost at the end of the block, and he turned to nod to his subordinates. They nodded back.

They ambled past the police car with two portly cops leaning on its bonnet, nodding to the demonstrators benignly. "Reinhardt" lowered his edge of the placard to the level of his torso, concealing his actions from onlookers. He glanced sideways at the riot police, who lolled in an alley some distance away and pulled out the pistol.

The first three rounds were harmless blanks, and "Reinhardt" fired them at the ground, holding the pistol close to his leg. On cue, one of his comrades fell to the ground, smearing his face with red paint from a tube carefully positioned inside his sleeve. "Reinhardt" then emptied the magazine in the direction of the riot police, firing through the placard. As he flung himself down, he saw two policemen collapse to the ground.

The street erupted in screams and mayhem. Demonstrators overwhelmed the cops next to the patrol vehicle, and "Reinhardt" saw with satisfaction that a burly, frenzied man wrestled a pistol from a cop and was trying to shoot the owner, clearly unfamiliar with the workings of a safety catch. Hiding his own gun inside the pocket, "Reinhardt" crawled over, pointing to the pistol as if trying to help - and when the man angled the butt of the pistol towards him, he thumbed the safety catch, pulled the slide, then wrenched the gun's barrel to point at the bearer. With the other hand "Reinhardt" got hold of the man's index finger and yanked it towards the handle. As his victim collapsed, "Reinhardt" pulled the pistol from a dying hand.

He now fired into the crowd, taking care not to aim where his comrades were busy pretending to assist the wounded. More shots

106

rang out overhead - it appeared that some police had taken the bait and returned fire. "Reinhardt" dropped to the ground and quickly crawled to the nearest body of a demonstrator.

He pushed his pistol into the dead hand and forced the limp index finger inside the trigger guard. He then lifted the nearest dead cop, using all of his strength to heft the heavy body off the ground and staggered forward towards the riot police with an hysterical expression on his face. Two ambulances screamed around the corner, skidding on tramway tracks, and one of the riot police frantically pointed towards them. "Reinhardt" nodded and increased his pace, moving as fast as he genuinely could.

An ambulance officer ran towards him and took the policeman's feet. The hurried towards the ambulance, where "Reinhardt" helped heave the body onto the trolley, then staggered away, doing his best to look like a shell-shocked citizen. Nobody challenged him, and he walked away, traversing a few city blocks. Certain of his safety, he turned into a malodorous alley between two restaurants and pushed a large dumpster to create hiding space.

Concealed by the smelly container, "Reinhardt" extracted a large switch-blade knife from its ankle sheath. With quick, certain movements he cut away the overalls and stuffed the rags into the dumpster. He dumped the beanie and peeled the skin-coloured latex gloves he wore all morning, dropping them on the ground. Those had to be discarded separately.

Under the overalls he wore crisp black pants and a dark turtle-neck skivvy, selected to conceal blood – which, to his surprise, proved unnecessary. One of his pockets yielded a string carry bag with a wad of cash and a packet of cloth wipes. He used those to remove all traces of a very productive morning from his face and neck, then wiped the latex powder off his hands. The gloves were placed into a plastic bag which was tucked into one of his socks.

A tall man of obvious wealth emerged from behind the dumpster and strode down the filthy alley, resplendent in designer travel gear. He turned into the busy street and marched into one of the Chinese restaurants open for yum cha. Positioning himself at a small table, he nodded to an old Chinese man who sat at the neighbouring table with a newspaper. The old man stared back gruffly, then returned to his reading.

When the waiter brought his beer, "Reinhardt" placed a few random orders from a small menu rather than await the trolleys. As the waiter left, he studied his hands with disapproval and arose, looking questioningly at a portly woman behind the cash register. She pointed to a grimy door at the back of the restaurant.

"Reinhardt" nodded his thanks and went where she indicated. He entered the male toilet and studied its peeling paint with disdain. Not finding what he wanted, he tried the female side – where he was rewarded with the sight of a large rubbish bin. He wrapped the plastic bag containing his gloves inside towel paper and shoved it deep into the bin.

He then washed his hands and dried them on more paper towels, wetting more and more of them until the bin was full. Satisfied that his detritus was buried out of sight, he returned to his table, now stacked with bamboo containers.

It was time for lunch.

###

"This thing is getting out of control," remarked Collins to no one in particular. As he said it, he became aware of the inanity of that statement and shrugged his shoulders angrily.

"Let's recap what we know," he ordered angrily. "Johny, you lead off."

John Marsden was an eager man, as Collins well knew. Not yet thirty, his Black Irish features and hazel eyes concealed a burning desire for promotion. He stood up, a tall man in neat dark trousers and a white shirt, a tie of conservative grey silk loose at his tanned neck.

"What we do know is this," began Marsden in a high voice that did not tie with his masculine appearance. "Shots are fired from the crowd, both on the riot squad and demonstrators. The latter show evidence of being killed at close range with Constable Turner's gun. Shots are fired in random directions. A 9mm Beretta found at the scene was used to fire on the riot squad, two of whom are hit, one fatally in the face and another in the shoulder. One of the riot boys returned fire, killing one demonstrator - one, unfortunately, who did not appear to be armed. The man found with the pistol appears to have been shot with Constable Turner's gun as well."

Collins shook his head.

"That's the messiest reconstruction of events I've ever heard."

Marsden coloured and began to fidget.

"Let's try this again, said Collins. "First, someone in the crowd fires on the riot squad from a Beretta."

Marsden nodded. Collins looked to the Asian man next to Marsden expectantly.

"That someone also shoots Constable Turner, takes his Glock and shoots a number of demonstrators at random, including the man found with the Beretta," said the Asiatic detective. "That doesn't make sense."

"What was the nature of that man's wound?" asked Collins.

Marsden leafed through the large sheath of documents in front of him and read for a few seconds.

"Chest, clean through the heart. So there is not much likelihood of him being shot, then taking the pistol from Constable Turner."

"Significant," said Collins. "I say it's a set-up. Let's start again."

"Someone fires on the riot squad, then the crowd surges and Constable Turner is attacked. He is overwhelmed, and his gun is taken. It is used to kill a number of demonstrators, then it is pushed into a dead man's hand. Four other demonstrators are killed by the riot squad returning fire. The perpetrators escape.

In addition, at least one man simulated a wound by smearing himself with theatre dye we found on the ground - presumably, to panic those around him. To sum up, the violence was staged by at least one man, most likely a larger number."

His subordinates sat still, staring at him intently. Collins turned away and stared out the panoramic window of the briefing room, many floors above ground level. The view, he noted in passing, was breathtaking - a sea of multicoloured lights that was Melbourne city in late dusk. It made Collins even angrier - the matter at hand simply did not belong in that landscape. He held on to that thought and rolled it around in his mind. Did not belong... Foreign?

"Cui bono?" he thought. The ancient question of all crime investigators.

"Who benefits?" he asked aloud.

"At first glance, one thing is obvious," said the Asian man confidently. "The shooting was deliberately staged to start a massacre. It does nothing for police reputation, that much is also evident - but it's unclear who would profit after that."

"Makes the unions look awfully bad," chimed in the dumpy woman from the corner. "Whatever points they tried to score over one dead thug on the picket line, it's now snowed under bad publicity, with accusations of irresponsibility and criminality flying from every newspaper column. Talkback radios are full of calls for the union movement to be banned from holding public gatherings. More than one government minister thundered about the full weight of the law, extensive investigations, royal commissions - none of this could possibly be what anyone in the union leadership wanted. I, for one, can't believe they could do something that could make them look this bad."

"My thoughts as well," said Collins, impressed. "What about a rogue group within the union?"

"Even less plausible," said Marsden bravely. "What about the theatre dye? That, surely, is the work of a professional. The gun - all wrong as well. A brand-new 9mm Beretta - an ordinary enough weapon in the underworld, but not one so flawlessly clean and recently oiled."

"That's true," agreed Collins. "It had none of the scratches and dents that you see on crims' guns."

"I can't see the stevedore company doing this either," continued Marsden, clearly on a roll. "An operation of this kind took many men to plan. I can't see anyone in their right mind involving more than a few of their trusted confidants in such a show. I can almost smell the management's glee at this turn of events - but there is simply not enough benefit to take such risks."

"That leaves us with a problem," rumbled Collins. "We had gone through the list of likely suspects. Who benefits, was the question. We don't have a plausible answer at all, which leaves investigators of the hottest case in the nation's history up shit creek. Are we agreed?"

He went back to the thought inspired by the pretty view. Foreign. Who? It would have to be a hostile party indeed. Islamic terrorism? Hardly - they would want everyone to know. Trade competitors? Ridiculous. Political interference.... But against unions - why? Someone on the opposite side of politics? CIA, MI6 - ridiculous again. He shook his head and decided against even voicing that thought.

"I have an idea," said Marsden. Collins stared at him expectantly.

"Let's search the footprints at the scene," said Marsden.

"Looking for?"

"A boot with glue in its sole."

"That is a valuable thought," whispered Collins, savouring it. "Same perpetrators....Wouldn't that make it interesting?"

Marsden picked up his cell phone, selected a number and stared at Collins, waiting for the connection.

"Billy," he said slowly. "We need to search the scene again. Remember that funny boot print from the picket line murder? Yes, the one with glue in the sole. Guess what I am looking for. Aha, now."

He hung up and nodded at Collins. "They have to wait till daylight, but will be on the scene first thing tomorrow. The forecast is for three days of dry weather.

"Very well," said Collins, exhaustion beginning to overtake him. "Anything else?"

He looked around, registering the same fatigue in every face.

"Time to go home, by the look of it," he told them. There was a grateful murmur as they gathered their papers and left. Collins turned away to avoid eye contact with Marsden.

As he collected the last of his belongings for the trip down to the car park, his phone chimed. Collins frowned and looked at the number. It came up as a line of zeroes, and he eagerly thumbed the call button.

"How are you, son?" he asked, the first positive emotion of the day colouring his voice with an unusual timbre.

"Dad, we are good," replied a sonorous voice, now tinged with a trace of the American rumble. "Nellie thinks she is pregnant."

Collins' face dissolved in a most rare of genuine, joyous smiles.

"Boy or girl?" he asked with delight.

"We will know in two weeks. She is not feeling all that good."

"Oh?"

"Just barfing, Dad. Nothing bad, but I am driving her to the lakes for Easter. I thought I would call now, in case the reception is bad."

"Thanks, Ryan," Collins closed his eyes hard squeezing the moisture from them. "You are a good kid."

"Happy birthday for Mum," said Ryan. "Are you very busy right now?"

"I am, son."

"Well, that's a good thing this time of year. Will you make it to the cemetery?"

"I will try, son. What I am working on is pretty

bad, but I think my leads are running out. Might lighten up by next week."

"Well, you know what I want, Dad."

"Yes," Collins whispered, his voice breaking with spasm. "Five red roses."

"And don't forget the bird seed."

"Yeah," said Collins shortly, nodding towards the city lights. "I won't."

"She loved native birds," said Ryan hoarsely. "I miss them too. There are hardly any birds here."

"I'll take care of it," said Collins, his voice regaining strength. "Give my love to Nellie, son. Be careful bouncing her around in that tank of yours."

"It's only a short ride from the freeway," Ryan chuckled. "Take care, Dad. We love you."

"I guess you won't be coming back this year," said Collins ruefully.

"Uh-uh. Your turn, anyway."

Collins sighed and turned away from the lights.

"I will see what can be done."

###

"Stupid fuck of a thing," mumbled Collins resignedly. He bent down and inspected a small scratch on the bumper of a compact Mercedes. "How am I supposed to see in here? She will have to wear it."

The pillars of the underground car park concealed his little misdeed from security cameras, and the bumper of the Mercedes was not virginal to begin with. A variety of cosmetic items in the dashboard tray indicated that the vehicle belonged to beauty-conscious female, who paid more attention to lipstick than to body work - and declaration of an accident in an unmarked car took a solid hour of paperwork. He sighed and told himself that he did not have such time to spare. In the interest of national security, the accident cannot be declared.

Having performed that dubious absolution, he pushed his bulk inside the car through a door he could only open half-way and reversed out of the narrow parking spot. He parked on a lower level where empty spaces abounded and trudged towards the lift, heavy briefcase in hand. He was dog-tired and felt many things, none of them pleasant - the ache from the gun holster against his ribs in an ever-tightening jacket, the gnawing pain in his worn hips, the stabbing sensation in his right knee, damaged when he was a much younger man. Collins chuckled at the memory - his tyre disintegrated in car chase, and he spent hours cramped in a wrecked car until it was cut into pieces to get him free.

The lift had arrived at last, and he rode it to the top floor of the hotel. He extracted the key card from his pocket and swiped it against his door irritably. It always took a few tries, and the more was one in need of a hot shower and a comfortable bed, the longer it took for the damn things to work.

Once inside, he set the briefcase next to the door and stepped out of his clothes, leaving them in a rumpled heap on the plush red carpet. He padded to the shower and spent the next ten minutes cleansing the remains of the day from his sallow skin. The bathroom mirror revealed an unflattering picture - shoulders that once bulged with muscle were now angled contours of bone. There was dimpled fat on his arms, and a round belly was topped by two sagging breasts. Collins shook his head in revulsion.

He threw the can of deodorant back in his wash bag and returned to the bedroom. He touched the button on the remote control on the bedside table and sat down on the bed, stretching the aching shoulders.

"Mr Reilly is awaited any moment now," said the reporter somewhat breathlessly. She was heavily dressed in a tweed coat and a silk scarf that complemented her sharp features to perfection.

"Shelley, do we have any idea about the

progress made?" asked the anchor, whose carefully coiffured head flashed up in the corner of the screen. "What is the mood over there?"

"Well, with the strike spreading from the ports into public transport and electricity, all parties have been very cautious with their statements," replied Shelley wistfully. "We had tried to obtain statements from a few people close to..."

Collins looked up as her voice trailed off into a sharp, unprofessional exclamation. The camera rocked as if the operator was nearly swept off his feet, then began to swing as he ran. The image was cut off abruptly, to be replaced by the coiffured anchor.

"It looks as if there are developments in the conference," he said importantly. "We are crossing to the lobby of the Federation Hotel now. Are you there, Shelley?"

"I am just making my way inside now, replied Shelley's still disembodied voice. "We are told that Mr Reilly is about to come down and make an announcement."

The anchor nodded and stared awkwardly for some seconds. Just as he pursed his lips to break the silence, the image was abruptly returned to the capacious leathery lobby of a city hotel. It was packed with reporters brandishing tape recorders and microphones, cameras on tripods, television lights and other paraphernalia of a dubious trade.

Shelley's camera operator evidently managed to fight his way to the front of the crowd, and he obtained an excellent view of the salient – burnished bronze doors of the lift. By unspoken agreement, the media scrum stopped a few metres short, leaving a small semicircle of floor space vacant.

The camera focussed on the numbers above the door. It showed the lift on the seventh floor. The crowd went silent as the lift began to move.

It stopped at the fifth floor, and the crowd muttered a collective disappointment. It went from there to the ninth floor, stayed an interminable length of time, then returned to the seventh floor and stayed there briefly.

The crowd watched in total silence as the lift rapidly traversed the numbers to the ground floor. There was a cheerful ping of the bell, and the bronze doors slid open.

Reilly was alone in the lift. He wore grey pinstriped pants, a perfect white shirt and a neat tie of blue silk, its knot loosened to the first button of his shirt. He looked tired and happy, and he held a paper coffee cup in his hand. There was an earnest smile on his round face.

He walked out of the lift with slow, precise steps of a fatigued man, taking off the steel-rimmed reading glasses and sliding them into the shirt pocket, where they joined an inexpensive fountain pen.

The media erupted in a chorus of shouts as he stopped before the cameras and waved his greeting. He waited for the cacophony to die down and raised his hand in supplication for silence.

"Mr Reilly," called out the intrepid Shelley. "Do you have good news?"

He nodded, the tired smile still playing on his lips.

"Good evening, everyone," he said with kind humour. "Especially to you, Shelley."

There were a few good-natured laughs. Shelley was known as one of his harshest critics.

"Good evening and good news," Reilly repeated in what was now an echoing silence."Good will and common sense had prevailed."

There was a loud cheer, which Reilly acknowledged with what passed for mild embarrassment. He raised his free hand again, sipping his coffee.

"Been a long day," he said apologetically, hiding the coffee cup from the cameras. "But I am pleased to report that we achieved an agreement, and the crisis is over. All parties had acknowledged that we live in uncertain times, and as a nation, we cannot afford to be divided in our purpose."

Applause broke out and acquired a certain rhythm. Reilly nodded, still smiling his tired smile. He raised his hand again, with a reluctance he failed to conceal fully.

"All strike action ends at zero-eight hundred tomorrow morning, " he announced. "The lockouts end one hour before, and everyone will return to work. In four weeks from now there will be another conference between all parties, which I will be chairing. I am hoping to resolve this matter without doing further damage to our national interests."

The applause broke out again and reached a tumultuous crescendo. Reilly nodded, clearly resisting an urge to bow.

When the noise died down, he stepped closer to the microphones, and his face filled the screen.

"Dear citizens of our great nation," he said in a strong voice, without a trace of smile or fatigue. "I want to make it very clear - this issue is about national integrity. It is quite above politics."

Collins sat on his bed, mesmerized.

"Cui bono," he whispered. "Fuck..."

He lowered his hand to the bedside table and snapped off the television.

"What?" he whispered to the dead screen. "What do I do now?"

Flynn Arnold liked to keep up the classic image of a police commissioner. It helped that he was a very large, heavily framed man with a square chin and huge, gnarled hands. The rest was constructed to fit the image - steel-grey hair cut very short, drooping handlebar moustache and a penetrating gaze from behind heavy eyelids that was supposed to stop criminals in their tracks.

He was, in fact, very blind without thick glasses - but tried not to wear them in the presence of others, to dispel the bookish look. The manner was all to form, world-wise serenity of an ageing Irish patriarch, punctuated with flashes of frightful but righteous anger. Among subordinates he cut a fatherly figure of a world-weary leader who was not averse to cutting a corner, a brooding, powerful warrior who is well aware of the limits of earthly power.

That rugged an haggard image did well to conceal a wily political operator. Arnold was now on a tight rope, with a long-serving conservative government about to topple after many years in office. A wind of change always boded ill for his organization, with power-hungry scumbags about to find themselves in charge of a wealthy country. Budgets would be rocked, and long-term projects would be abandoned in favour of wild goose chases. Some white elephants would be nurtured, and some would be euthanased. Like all experienced public servants, Arnold was not a fan of change, and he didn't think much of democracy either.

One habit that was not finely tuned to exemplary discharge of his duties was a terminal addiction to tobacco. Owing to tranquillizing properties of nicotine, police and military personnel are always the last to be cured of such affliction, and many, if not most, of Arnold's subordinates still smoked. All but he, however, were able to keep that habit out of their daily work. Entering and leaving office buildings in which Federal Police does most of its work had long been encumbered by protracted security procedures, and smoking on the job is most impractical.

Arnold's addiction, however, knew no such constraints. Upon appointment to his exalted position he moved the Commissioner's office to a higher floor, where a few rooms had inexplicable access to small balconies. Arnold made his office in one such room, adorning the balcony with a single implement - a large stone pot, into which he tossed empty butts. Much useful business was conducted in the proximity of that urn, away from the buzz of telephones and computers. Even more amazingly, no objections ensued from politically correct Nazis, which enhanced Arnold's reputation even further.

There was an even better reason to conduct business on the balcony - it was difficult to listen to conversations. The wind and traffic noise made local bugs difficult to operate. A parabolic microphone capable of picking up voices hundreds of metres away was not out of the question, but the operator would have to conceal himself on a hill covered with dead grass that faced the headquarters. The risk of being overheard was therefore acceptably small.

Arnold stood over the urn with a snarl frozen on his face. The cigarette in his right hand was gathering a long head of ash, and it was not receiving much attention.

"No, fuck it, no, no, no and no!" he shouted, stabbing the hapless cigarette in the direction of his nemesis. The ash fell off and rolled over the edge of the balcony.

"I am going to stand here and repeat what I have to say until you address my arguments," replied Collins in a cold, even tone. "We found the same boot print at both scenes. A foreign brand not available for sale in Australia. This is a professional operation, clearly designed to create political trouble."

"I am buying that part."

"Who benefits, is the next question. Answer that, and you solve just about any crime."

"Yes."

"One clear beneficiary is our next Prime Minster. He steps into the strike like a messiah, and the problem evaporates. You have to be a true believer to swallow that, and there are no believers here."

"Off the record," said Arnold, holding his cigarette like a traffic baton.

"Fine," replied Collins with utter lack of enthusiasm.

He was one of the new wave - a senior officer past retirement age that was recently made illegal. Politicians finally realized that the old-age bomb was a non-event - the modern "elderly" neither need, nor wish to retire. Few modern workers reaching retirement age are broken by a lifetime of manual labour, and their work capacity declines ever so slowly - largely offset, until late seventies, by acquisition of experience and general understanding of life. On the other side of the ledger, the economics of retirement pressure people to remain at work.

In the public service such people soon became prized for another quality - they were genuinely without fear of favour. Their pension is guaranteed and available on demand, unless they commit a crime in office. That pension is not means-tested, which allows them to pick up lucrative contracts - even in the same public service, effectively doubling their income. In his study at home Collins stowed a thick folder of offers from security companies and more than a few government agencies who couldn't wait for him to "retire".

That made the very tone of the present conversation possible, and it also made Collins an irritant that could not be removed. The unspoken threat was that he could take his problem to a higher office - and even the media - with few personal consequences. That was an entirely unanticipated effect of removing compulsory retirement.

Arnold lit another cigarette from the first, inhaled and slowly blew out the smoke, tossing the glowing butt into the urn.

"Look, Jim," he began with a gesture of supplication. "You just can't barge into the highest office in the land and interrogate the man who is five minutes past becoming a Prime Minister. It's just not done."

"Whitlam," came the immediate reply. "Who was lucky he didn't end up doing time."

"A very long time ago," countered Arnold. "Look, we are a middle-weight power these days. Things are so much more complicated."

"But you are still not allowed to kill people for political advantage - or am I wrong?"

"Look at the practicalities, Jim. Let's say he actually did this - what evidence are you hoping to uncover?"

"No idea, Commissioner. Like any old-fashioned crime investigation - get a few leads, follow them, focus on suspects, shake them down and see what falls out of their pockets. I don't give a shit what the main suspect does for a living."

"But he is not going to crack, Jim. Before you get near shaking him down, he will shut down half the government, don't you see - you will be off to Thailand to do drug liaison with local cops who make millions from selling drugs, and I will be retired at home, watching daytime soaps and lucky if not subjected to some kind of harassment. You know this bunch - they are great operators and they know how to hate. And I bet they thought it through. You really think they used local talent that you could bundle into a petty wagon?"

"Unlikely," replied Collins with diminished

aggression. "I would suspect they imported someone. Winchester-like."

Arnold flinched at the embarrassing reminder. Winchester was an assistant commissioner, who was assassinated in office two decades before. A bumbling local psychopath was scapegoated for what was clearly a professional hit - two shots to the head in the darkness, the assassin disappearing without a trace.

No one especially cared about the psychopath spending the rest of his life in jail - he had something of a bad reputation and not a single friend. But one thing was clear to any sensible observer - the real killer left no loose ends. Most likely, he flew into the country, did the job and flew out just as investigators began their impossible job.

"Even more so," said Arnold. "You don't really expect our new and great leader to start crying and confess, do you? Imagine the interrogation - his legal team won't fit into the lift. You won't even be able to make eye contact."

"You can leave that to me," said Collins. "You know I won't be unnerved, and you know that he will be."

"Perhaps. But what were you planning to ask? Where were you at nine o'clock last Friday? What's this blood on the hammer in your garage? Come on, admit it, honourable member for Fraser - you had a man killed on a picket line and then fired shots into the crowd of demonstrators to win an election? Fuck, Jim – use your common sense."

"But you don't expect me to just leave it, surely."

"Ah," Arnold frowned, sucked on the remains of his cigarette and threw it in the urn. "Off the record and strictly off the record - yes, I do."

Collins stared, then shook his head in sadness.

"It's a wrong that I don't think we can right," explained Arnold. Eight murders, sure - but I don't think you can get to him if he's the man."

"I just can't believe you are saying this. Commissioner. How can you even say this so calmly?"

"I've had a lifetime to get used to such outrages," said Arnold, lighting another cigarette. "What I had come to realize is that our elected representatives kill citizens like flies, and it's not even illegal. Look over there."

His stubby index finger traced a path in the air. Collins followed it and saw a distant freeway that wound itself past the pine plantation.

"See that intersection?" asked Arnold.

Collins instantly knew what he meant. It was a cloverleaf junction of a freeway with a road that pierced the forest, and one of the entrances onto the freeway had an incorrect camber. There was a good dozen of accidents there every winter - anyone who entered the freeway with a slight excess of speed was liable to slide into the path of speeding traffic. The local government refused to close the intersection and it debated the problem with each change of minister. Alas, the likely cost defeated the proposal on each occasion.

"Four people died there in the past twelve months," echoed Arnold. "As good as if that fuckwit who runs the transport department came along with a gun and shot them - but totally legal and above board."

Collins nodded thoughtfully.

"And that's just one little bit of road," continued Arnold. "What about ignition immobilizers - how many more years do we have to wait before they become compulsory?"

Collins nodded again. He was an ardent fan of devices that locked vehicle ignition when alcohol fumes were detected near the driver's seat. It was argued that a good spray-painter's mask would defeat them, but Collins couldn't see an average citizen to have the stomach for such measures - and anyone seeing the driver wearing breathing apparatus would instantly know what they were up to. The measure was long-shown to be a major saver of lives overseas, yet no Australian jurisdiction had even talked about making them compulsory.

"All true," said Collins. "But I had never gave up on such a likely suspect in my entire life, and I don't intend to now."

Arnold sensed the wind and changed tack.

"I am not actually advising you to give up. What I am saying is this - whatever you are going to do, it has to stick."

"That goes without saying," said Collins. "I wasn't planning on hammering Reilly tomorrow. I came here to discuss and to plan."

"That's more like it," Arnold grinned broadly. "Let's go inside."

Stockley was a very handsome man aged around fifty. His face bore a certain resemblance to a famous actor - a tall forehead, long aquiline nose and dark hair that maintained thickness in middle age. The figure was fine too - not very distinguished, but entirely free of flab. The lift's mirror reassured that he made a superb clothes horse.

His job, on the other hand, was a different

matter. There was one problem after another in his agency, for some time a mere token remainder of a toothy organization that once chased KGB out of Australia. Now reduced to eavesdropping on the ravings of unemployed mullahs, it was a difficult outfit to take seriously. Performance, morale and budgets all reflected this loss of purpose.

The new government was neither help nor hindrance, as far as Stockley was concerned. A few such governments came and went on his watch, and he was well used to the routine. Every now and again he was blamed for missing something, and that required speedy footwork and an even faster mouth. Stockley was well-endowed with both and did not mind these occasional outbreaks of bad weather. They kept him in shape and were over quickly enough, allowing his department to return to masterful inactivity under the clement sun.

He readjusted the knot of yellow silk and straightened the lapels of his black suit that matched his complexion to perfection. The Piaget watch complemented the shining gold of his wedding ring, and Italian loafers glowed like two elegantly curved mirrors. The security tag was the sole eyesore, hanging around his neck on a cheap nylon cord. Its photo was all wrong as well, but this was a concession to ugly reality, an exception that merely proved the rule.

The lift stopped, and Stockley strolled down

the corridor carpeted in plush green. He crossed two sets of glass doors that were opened by swiping his security tag across the locks.

The Prime Minister's receptionist was a mousy woman in a plain black dress. She was quite young and even pretty, noted Stockley, but the hair was all wrong, brown streaks showing through a cheap dye job. He stared at her with disapproval that she instantly found disconcerting. That too had a useful effect.

"I will just..." she stammered, lifting the receiver. Stockley nodded his head imperially, not bothering to sit down.

Nuances are everything, he thought as Stahl emerged from the carved wooden door, face creasing in a rare smile of apology. Someone who walked in with a neutral expression would have been kept waiting far longer.

Stockley sank into the proffered leather armchair and leaned back luxuriantly. There was a superb view of the mountains, he noted - the haze of recent bushfires was almost gone. The world was a perfect place that late morning, and the weekend was not far away either.

Reilly put down the coffee mug and hastily wiped the blonde moustache with his sleeve, making Stockley wince as if he was struck.

"How goes the world, David?"

Stockley winced again from the use of his first name, which he especially disliked.

"All in all," he replied in his measured, musical rhythm. "Not too badly. I am here to discuss a relatively small matter, Prime Minister."

He waited until the length of his silence made it clear that the matter was not small.

"It's about the latest file requisition," continued Stockley. He extracted a printed list from the inside pocket of his jacket. "These are the files your office had asked for, Prime Minister."

"Ah," Stahl affected something of an embarrassed grimace. "Those files."

Stockley played the statue of a civil service mandarin to the hilt, staring forward with an expression that was attention, courtesy, disapproval and bemusement in equal, carefully measured, parts.

"We are attending to some internal business," explained Stahl. "There are certain rumours which we intend to clear up."

"But surely my department is no mere library," replied Stockley, his tone now two parts disapproving tutor, one part caring mentor. "If there is a problem, sirs, all you needed to do was bring it to our attention."

"Surely," chimed O'Reilly peaceably. "But when there are accusations about one's predecessors, there is such a need to avoid the look of a vendetta."

Stockley spent the next three seconds sitting perfectly still as his brain dashed a marathon beneath a crop of dark hair.

To his knowledge, the present administration had no pressing need to settle any scores. Still, the comrades were good haters, he allowed with grace. A small thing it may be to a detached observer, but no debt ever goes unpaid. Consistently and reliably – one can say that much for their breed of scavenger.

"Indeed," he replied in a matching tone. "It would not be good form for my department to be seen as running such errands. If, of course, it is certain that they are outside our purview."

Safe enough, he breathed hard at the end of the marathon. If they find the slightest whiff of bad, those mongrels will drag it through every official instance anyway. No one fucks with their kind and expects a quiet retirement later.

"Oh," Stahl smiled his best hyena grin. "Should any allegations ever match documented facts, your lads will have no choice but get involved."

"Not that we hunger for business," Stockley eased the conversation from fencing to amiable banter. "New Zealand and all..."

Smiles broke out all around. Only a week before the nature lovers, recently elected to run New Zealand, found themselves kicked out of the ANZUS alliance for broadcasting a few inconvenient facts. The said facts were some of the worst-kept secrets on the planet, but Americans made it the last straw and took serious offence. All over Canberra carefully plucked eyebrows went up in club lounges and office tea rooms. Boffins locked wits in contest, trying to predict the subject of the next comedy on the other side of the Tasman. Stockley's department found that picnic a welcome diversion from trying to forestall Islamist rabble-rousing in Sydney.

"Thank you, Prime Minister," continued Stockley, now a sage ministering to admiring commoners. "That leaves just one specific point of concern."

He leaned towards the table and planted a manicured index finger on a single entry on his list. Reilly leaned forward to confirm it.

"Damn thing," he replied with a disapproving frown. "A very ugly allegation, that one. A certain rumour about a senior man, later one of our MP's. The mutt is said to have tried to sell sensational stuff to some writer. Fortunately, the latter refused to use it and came to one of our people instead. Keep it in the family, kind of thing."

Stockley's eyebrows went up in genuine puzzlement.

"But there is only one copy of this file, Prime Minister," he replied in his real voice, now all business. "It has never been requisitioned since it was archived. I checked this myself."

"Not requisitioned officially," corrected Stahl.

"Just a moment," said Stockley firmly. "We are talking about a leak from my agency. We should have been informed."

"No, not from your agency," said Stahl, shaking his head with mirth.

"No other instrumentality was involved in this business." protested Stockley, struggling to recall the hearsay about events at the dawn of his career.

"No, I am afraid there were a few others," replied Reilly with a crease of distaste, carefully constructed with his lips alone. He took another sip of coffee and stabbed at the sheet with a fine index finger. "There were, in fact, multiple agencies which were very involved but created no departmental records. We are certain that the leak did not come from intelligence."

"But that is still no political football," said Stockley firmly. "The Federal Police must become involved, at the very least."

"If only," said Reilly dreamily. "Wouldn't that be a tempting way to secure one of our looser canons. But first we need to confirm that allegations have substance – otherwise it's a case of being careful what you wish for. This only landed on my desk recently, and I want to see if the documents match the allegations. Very much."

Recently, mused Stockley. Who the hell would take interest in this stuff recently?

"Prime Minister," he said firmly. "I am of the opinion, sir, that any matter regarding these events should be investigated through official channels. Even if the subject of the inquiry is of no current interest to my department."

"But then, David, I would have to surrender my source," explained Reilly. "That would be a gross breach of faith. Not to mention that the source would then clam up and refuse to cooperate with the inquiry. A wrong-doer could get off scot-free as a result of a boots-and-all approach."

Stockley winced with resignation. It was a mundane matter of fact - his present political master came from an organization that had direct dealings with criminals on a daily basis.

No union was complete without thugs and enforcers. Turf wars in that fraternity were settled with crowbars rather than citations from Marx.

It was time to surrender with dignity.

"Then you are surely correct, Prime Minister," the wavy coiffure was even seen to waver in a small bow. "You will, I have no doubt, deal with these allegations with your customary logic and propriety."

Reilly slowly nodded with his best Sometimes-the-World-Is-Too-Much expression.

"All right, David," he uttered, studying the bottom of the coffee mug with sadness. "Seeing that you are already here, tell us about New Zealand. What the fuck were they thinking?"

"You are a lethally hard man to get near," said Klimov, smiling impeccably. "I was beginning to get desperate."

"You can thank the previous administration for budget constraints," Stahl nodded with a wooden smile of his own. "My predecessor had a full round-the-clock security circus. I, at least, can come here in peace."

They were finally alone, standing in the courtyard of Stahl's favourite Italian restaurant. It was drizzling, and other smokers sensibly postponed satisfying their cravings - which they, in any case, were long accustomed to postpone by a myriad of regulations against smoking. The tide had turned, and they found themselves a rare species in modern politics - a group that can be persecuted not only with impunity, but also with benefit to the persecutor.

Stahl studied the tip of his small cigar, still glowing despite the drizzle, and he took a reluctant puff. Stahl refused to admit that he gave up - but in truth and like all sensible people, he was well over the taste that went with the habit. Smelling cigar smoke was one thing, but sucking on the vile things that emanated it was quite another. One may enjoy all kinds of smells, after all, without the slightest desire to taste their sources. Alas, the cigar kept going out unless he kept puffing, and allowing it a peaceful death would interfere with his cover.

"Did you bring what I asked?" asked Klimov genially.

"It's here."

"Was there any trouble?"

"Stockley came over in full regalia to demand why we wanted your file. We told him that we were checking facts in preparation for a small bloodletting within the party."

"And he accepted that without checking?" asked Klimov with some amazement.

"Apparently. Mind, when we bleed one of our own, it pays to stay away if you possibly can."

"Very well then," said Klimov, pointing at yellow bottlebrush with his cigarette, as if making idle conversation. "Let's trade. Drop the card at the door, just next to the pot filled with cigarette ends. When my wife and I leave, we will say goodbye to you formally. During our handshake a small ladies' phone will drop into your sleeve. Bring up your other hand to mine and hold onto it after I let go. Whatever you do, don't drop it for everyone to see. Don't show it to anyone and keep it in a safe place. It takes a standard USB charger, and I had prepaid an hour of talk time. It is not traceable, but delete my messages and call logs as soon as you memorize my number."

"What is that for?" asked Stahl, intently studying the intricate petals of the bottlebrush.

"It will be necessary to convey further instructions," Klimov told him, smiling radiantly. "Laugh, you idiot. People are looking at us."

Stahl overrode a surge of anger to mimic hearing something moderately amusing and smutty.

"What fucking instructions?"

"You must destroy the paper file," explained Klimov. "Otherwise it will be possible to trace what happened and hence your involvement. For which you will need my fucking instructions, as you care to call them. Otherwise you will fuck up and get caught, as I care to call it."

Stahl nodded angrily.

"There is a simple way to make a delayed pyrotechnic charge and incinerate papers inside a safe," continued Klimov. "Looks like an electrical malfunction afterwards. The computer record must also be destroyed, although that's a lot easier,"

"How am I supposed to delete classified computer records?"

"There is a chap in your support staff by the name of John Casey. He will be detained by a traffic patrol tomorrow night - a bit of erratic driving, I am afraid, not a very high alcohol level, but he will be facing charges all the same. You will read about it in The Canberra Times the next day and summon him in for a tête-a-tête, as a concerned boss. Don't be too hard on him and give him access to your secure terminal. He will work quickly and without leaving a trace. Alas, I fear, he won't be showing up for the hearing. I am given to understand that he misses his family and snow - on both counts he will be pleased to conclude his tour of duty in your country."

Stahl looked up, impressed. A sleeper right inside the Prime Minister's Department, he thought. In IT security, no less — and one of how many? Best not to think about it; just as well that his people are no longer our real enemies.

"Now let's do the card," said Klimov, still smiling.

Stahl nodded and turned with a short "see you in there" nod. He returned to the door, crushed his cigar in the pot filled with dry soil and let a small plastic square drop from his other hand onto the tiles.

Klimov finished his cigarette, still contemplating the delicate whorls of the bottlebrush, then turned to the entrance. He waved to Raisa with a radiant smile and bent down to crush his cigarette in the same pot. He then turned slightly to attend to a loose shoelace, picking up the tiny plastic box from the wet tiles and deftly slipping it into his shoe. It contained a memory card, all being well, filled with intact and readable images of Morozov's file.

###

Two large 4WD's bounced over the last of the night's obstacles. It was some feat in the dead of the night, with only the dim moonlight to guide them across deep ruts, fallen trees and the odd rock fall. The occupants left the vehicles with barely a sound and gently pressed the doors shut, preserving the night's peace. On a sign from their leader they fanned out into a loose formation and began to move downhill, towards a shack nestled in the trees.

Less than an hour later one of them walked through a thin line of nylon, tearing it off the anchor on a sturdy white gum. Fifty yards away a weight fell freely to the ground. It pulled a small switch attached to a radio beacon that instantly came to life, sending a signal to a receiver in the house.

Morozov woke up to a gentle chime next to the pillow and stretched out to silence the alarm. He had rehearsed the routine on every occasion when a stray kangaroo broke on of his perimeter lines. There were no exceptions - especially now.

He rolled out of bed, avoiding the square of moonlight thrown on the floor through the window. He crawled across the width of the shack and reached the closet with emergency gear. He quickly dressed away from the moonlight and stole towards the back door, a small backpack on his shoulders and a hunting rifle in his hands.

The pack contained credit cards, a large quantity of ammunition, a camouflage-coloured anorak and an empty plastic bottle, to be filled from the spring at the bottom of the hill. There was a spare set of clothes - casual, indistinct attire - and a small package in a watertight aluminium case.

Having stopped to listen for sounds of intrusion, he slipped out the back door and pressed it shut without making a sound. He stayed in the shadow of large trees, sprinting across the faded lawn into a clump of bushes where he waited, heart pounding against his chest. He let his breathing settle and waited for the adrenaline to dissipate into icy predawn air. He settled into the dense undergrowth and hid, scanning the expanse of the hill by the light of the huge, yellow moon.

A few minutes later excitement began to burn the pit of his stomach. A blundering kangaroo usually continued to crash through the bush, clearly identifying itself as such. This time was different, he realized, as faint rustling continued to drift across from the treeline. It appeared to grow louder, and he waited in the bushes, completely still and silent, clutching the rifle in sweating hands.

His discipline was rewarded - he felt, long before seeing, their presence. Four men appeared from the darkness and slid past Morozov without making a sound, which terrified him. His fear reached a peak when he saw that they were armed with machine pistols, held with professional ease. Morozov watched them surround the house and waited until one of them dove through the window, the sound of shattering glass savagely tearing the night silence.

Some minutes later the man came out of the front door, gesturing the others inside. He took off his ski mask: blond hair shone in the bright moonlight as he wiped sweat from his forehead. Others went inside, and Morozov saw more men, whose presence he did not even suspect, emerge from the bush to join them.

Morozov slid out of the bushes, invisible in his dark clothing. He managed to cover the distance to the edge of the forest in total silence and dropped to the ground as soon as he reached the trees. His back burning with an expectation of a bullet, he gasped for breath as he crawled away from the moonlight. Fresh clothing was drenched in sweat when he reached cover, sliding behind the trunk of a gnarled red gum.

Morozov undid the clasp at his chest to drop the backpack and reached inside it without lowering his gaze from the moonlit expanse of dead grass, which separated him from the intruders. The aluminium box shimmered in the moonlight as he opened the lid and carefully retrieved one of the small objects it contained.

He carefully opened the bolt of his rifle, catching the round that was jerked from the chamber. Holding it in his mouth, he slipped the object from the case into the rifle chamber and closed the bolt.

Less than ten minutes later the raiding party emerged from the house. Coming through the door one by one, they presented a cluster of targets on the veranda. Morozov was no expert sniper, but years of living in the hills left him bereft of other entertainment. He was now quite proficient with stationary targets.

He appraised the wind - virtually absent - then calculated the amount of drop for a low-power charge. A small cloud drifted over the moon, but he was content to wait until the ghostly light returned.

He inhaled deeply, exhaled half-way and closed his mouth, trapping air to stiffen his torso as he was taught decades before. He took careful aim, corrected the height and gently squeezed the trigger. The sharp report of the rifle echoed across the hill.

The attackers dove for cover and scanned the bushes, looking for movement. None came - Morozov was long gone, running down the hill towards the river.

"Reinhardt" ran a hand across his thigh, feeing a trickle of fresh blood from the tiny wound. Klimov crawled towards him and examined the hole in the fabric by the light of a tiny torch held in his mouth.

"Shotgun pellet?" he suggested.

"Surely not, Comrade Colonel," replied the blond man, running his fingers over the leg experimentally. "There was nowhere near enough noise or impact for a shotgun. Most likely, I fell on a sharp stick. Think nothing of it."

"Have it checked when we return," ordered Klimov, his eye still scanning the treeline. He still couldn't tell where the shot came from. No one else had moved, his men continuing to scan the horizon to no avail. Looking at the still vegetation, he made a decision and rose to his feet.

"Up," he said briskly." He's gone."

"Maybe he is headed towards town, said someone.

"Most likely," agreed Klimov. "Let's see if we can head him off."

When they returned to their cars, they found both of them slumped on slashed tyres - one each.

"He can't be far," said "Reinhardt", wistfully looking at the dense bush. "We may be able to find him if we follow quickly."

"No," Klimov shook his head with vigour. "You don't know this country or its conditions, but he lived here for many years. He would have mapped his escape route to perfection. Change the tyres, then we'll split up and see if we can head him off on the road."

It was nearing dawn, with the edge of light ghosting the taller hilltops. As his subordinates busied themselves with spare wheels, Klimov stared intently at the map. It seemed to him that unless Morozov chose to waste much time and energy in steep and densely wooded terrain, there were only two directions to choose from - up or down along the river. Placing an ambush at each end of the valley was as good a chance of cutting him off as they had now.

He was wrong. Morozov used the last hours of darkness to locate an overgrown fire track. It was far too rough for modern vehicles and judged too unsafe as an escape route for men trapped by fire. A large mound of boulders was piled at its entrance, and the track was allowed to return to its natural state. Overshadowed by tall trees, it was long-gone from aerial photographs - and hence, modern maps.

Yet despite a vicious gradient it could still be navigated with relative speed on foot. A determined pedestrian now did exactly that, making good progress in the northerly direction. The bush was very dense near the ridge line, and one could stand on top of whoever one hunted without being aware of it.

Klimov's men spent a frustrating morning, sweating in two ambush positions at either end of the valley. Meanwhile Morozov climbed over the first Alpine ridge and began a long downward trek to the highway.

He was a little tired but not in the least interested in resting. His dreams were dreadful of late, and the longer he slept, the more vivid they became. They were all variations on the same theme, the same nightmare that drove him to a desperate flight three decades before. It bothered him often in the last few weeks.

Rebirth Island, a name that became one of Soviet Union's greatest ironies, is a flat expanse of sand at the northern end of Aral Sea. Most of Morozov's dreams began with a huge storm cloud that arose over the water and smashed into the low, sand-coloured buildings on the island.

Morozov would try to run, but the windows of the laboratory building shattered one by one, peppering the back of his neck with razor-sharp icicles. He would tear off the blood-soaked lab coat to cover his nose and mouth, but the sharp tang of laboratory chemicals told him it was too late.

It meant that the vials had shattered, and tiny harbingers of death blew over the dry sand covered with sparse vegetation. He would stop running and walk aimlessly, reaching the desolate beach before sunset. Then it was time to lie down on the sand and wait for the fever.

Sometimes the dream varied, and the beach was strewn with bodies in red overalls. A boatload of condemned criminals arrived once a month for "special duties". In the dream it ran aground in the storm, and the prisoners panicked, trying to swim ashore. They were shredded by heavy-calibre fire from patrol boats, bloody remains washing up all over the beach. Morozov would bend down to stare into unseeing eyes, thinking that they were lucky to be killed here, rather than chained to the bunk in the isolation block.

Sometimes infected men took a long time to die, and they had to be shot with cyanide darts from a special hatch in the wall. Ordinary firearms, even low-calibre, left too much infectious gore on the walls.

Hauling bodies to the incinerator in the centre of the island was the least favourite job in the complex. It could not be delegated because only the scientists could be trusted to make no mistakes. They alone understood the consequences in full.

Morozov began to sweat as he approached the distant highway. The sticky feeling under the arms reminded him of the putrid moisture inside the rubber suit. He was always aware of that moisture as he unlocked the handcuffs from a dead wrist still burning with fever. He then had to manoeuvre the body into a rubber bag, held open by an assistant.

They would drop the corpse onto a plywood trolley with wooden wheels, preparing to haul it out of the cell. Morozov remembered how he had to seal the door behind them, by turning a heavy metal wheel. His assistant would throw the switch to activate formaldehyde sprinklers, to wipe out any trace of life from the zinc-lined bunker. While the chemicals did their work, they would wheel the trolley down the long corridor, then trudge along a concrete roadway towards the centre of the island.

The incinerator was never shut down. They would slide a heavy steel door and give the trolley the final push down a long, sloping corridor. The fire hatch at the bottom would swivel open, receiving the load with an extra burst of welcoming flame. Then it was time to hose the suits with formaldehyde and strip, leaving them to dry in the burning sun.

The rest of the day after such duties was designated as rest. They would swim in the salty Aral Sea and drink laboratory alcohol in the shade behind the residential block. Intoxication was strictly against the rules, but modest consumption was condoned in these circumstances.

Occasionally the ageing rubber cracked and leaked; this only became known once the stench of formaldehyde penetrated the suit. The next week would be spent in quarantine - a wooden shack at the far end of the island, downwind from the rest of the complex. The occupant would pass the time drinking nothing stronger than beer and measuring his temperature on the hour.

The shack was supplied with cyanide capsules, in case the temperature began to climb. It was deliberately constructed from highly combustible plywood - if the occupant failed to respond to the sentry's calls, it would be set on fire with an incendiary round, from a distance.

Morozov clocked up three weeks inside that shack, and the last stint broke him completely. Anxiety made him feel as if he had a fever, and after a while he no longer believed the thermometer readings. After his request for sedatives was denied, he caught himself eyeing the sealed metal box with cyanide capsules. That terrified him more than the hourly measurements. He was afraid to go to sleep, terrified to miss the twice-daily call from the guard. He would rush outside as the soldiers backed away, assault rifles at the ready. Morozov would put up his hands in mock surrender and collect the food, left on the sand nearby.

He would clown around, asking for black caviar and foreign vodka, but in truth he was terrified. At the end of the third stint in the shack he began to think the unthinkable.

Resignation was not an option - he knew that from the day he set foot on Rebirth Island. Given what he knew, it was most unlikely that he would ever be allowed to return to what passed for any kind of normal life. Dirty secrets of the criminal state were far more important than his insignificant life - especially as he was complicit in its worst crime. Morozov could not think of any men who left the complex - the scientific personnel appeared to consist of single males who were assigned to Rebirth Island for life. Admittedly, none of them voiced a desire to leave, but then they would hardly vocalize such thoughts.

Suicide was the next obvious option. Strangely, Morozov could only think of one such instance - an older biochemist diagnosed with lung cancer. Even a crude X-Ray available on the island was able to show that his disease was inoperable, and the next day he was found hanging from a sturdy overhead pipe in the showers. No one questioned his exit - it seemed a logical thing to do.

There was just one other way, and Morozov agonized about it for many weeks after being released from the quarantine shack. He thought it over as thoroughly as he ever thought in his life. The skeleton of the idea gradually took on flesh until no apparent detail was left to chance.

Morozov volunteered to serve on a committee that made contingency plans – mainly scenarios of experimental disease being transmitted to the local population. That gave him unfettered access to detailed military maps, all the way to the southern border.

He was once taught that no battle plan survives the first shots of battle - but his escape plan unfolded perfectly. He carried it out with ruthless and relentless precision, racing ahead until he reached safety - or so it appeared then.

Morozov quickened his pace as the track began to level out - it was important that he made the highway before sunrise. His plan was to board a truck, slowed to a crawl on a steep hill nearby. He would ride that truck to the regional centre, where a series of roundabouts and traffic lights made it possible to jump off at slow speed. That could only happen when few people were about.

As he positioned himself in a clump of bushes next to the highway, he wondered whether Rebirth Island still operated today. Morozov's breath froze at the thought that what he had just set in motion may culminate in his return to the quarantine shack for one final time.

###

"Just a moment," said Collins and flipped open his phone.

"Boss," he heard Marsden's voice. "Something came up."

"I am listening," explained Collins irritably.

He studied the man sitting opposite. Old fox McGovern looked as genuine as a three-dollar note. Whether over this or something else, he had reason to fear the long arm of the law. The posture gave it away all by itself - McGovern sat in a comfortable office chair as if expecting Collins to jump over his desk and throttle him with bare hands.

"That footprint," said Marsden. "We got another match."

"Is that so?" replied Collins harshly, feeling his heart quicken to a hunting beat. A straight line cannot be reliably drawn through two points that are close to each other - but a third point further away makes the direction of such line certain.

"That file came from Victoria Police," said Marsden. "A local hunter in the hills near Purple Creek heard a whole lot of shots two nights ago. He is ex-Iraq, and he recognized weapons of Eastern European manufacture by sound. Had the good sense to hide in the bush, then he walked out to his car and made the report. They swept the scene yesterday, and the file was uploaded today. The image matcher detected a similarity in boot prints, and it turns out to be correct."

"Where is that place?" Collins glared at the union leader, but the latter did not appear as if he heard Marsden. Just in case, Collins pressed the phone tighter to his ear. It would have been better to go back to his car, but this was no time to break eye contact.

"Eastern Victoria," said Marsden. "Nearest centre is Bairnsdale, but it's nowhere, really. It's not a town, just a map name for a cluster of properties in the foothills."

"Are you in the office?" asked Collins.

"In my car at Albert Park Mall, having lunch."

"Don't move," ordered Collins. "I will call back."

He shut off the phone and smiled apologetically at McGovern.

"The quicker you tell me everything you know, the less trouble you are in," said Collins in a fatherly manner.

"There is only one small thing," said McGovern with a sharp intake of breath. "Look, this was a totally legitimate protest."

Collins nodded encouragement.

"The whole thing was legit," repeated McGovern. "The strike, the picket, the march. Except this one little thing."

Collins nodded sagely.

"Someone said there will be trouble."

"Who?"

"I got a call from one of the organizers, a man called Steiner. I remember because he emigrated from Austria, and he is hard to understand. He said there were reports of possible provocation and advised that the marchers get kitted up. You know, bike helmets, thick jackets, face shields, that kind of thing."

"But there was none of that crap at the march," said Collins. "Why did you disregard that information?"

"I bounced it off a few people, and they were real unhappy. Wanted to call off the march, even. So I called Steiner back to ask a few questions."

"What did he say?"

"He replied that he knew nothing about it. I believed him - the man I called had a totally different accent. Still hard to understand, but I could hear the difference right away. His voice was much higher, too."

"Did you report it?"

"Seemed no point to it," said McGovern ruefully. "We copped a lot of crap since the whole thing started. Cliff's murder, I mean. I decided it was just a bit of sabotage."

Collins nodded in thought.

"I will be in touch," he said, rising heavily. "You hear or think of anything else, you let me know. If I find out you withheld something, I'll shove my arm up your arse and turn you inside out. Promise."

McGovern nodded pathetically.

"One more thing," said Collins. He put two large hands with scarred knuckles on McGovern's desk and leaned down, staring menacingly. "Could this have anything to do with the federal election?"

McGovern broke into fresh sweat and recoiled, as if a snake was thrust across his desk.

"Oooh," he whispered in fright. "Now I see what you are after..."

"Because if it does," rasped Collins, eyes boring at McGovern from beneath bunched eyebrows. "If it does, it's time for you to choose sides."

McGovern did not react.

"Yes, sides," repeated Collins. He pointed to the large Australian flag in the corner of the office. "You can choose that side or you can choose another."

McGovern shook his head frantically and opened his mouth in protest.

"Keep your lying mouth shut and listen," hissed Collins viciously. "I don't want words. I want you to think through the consequences and act accordingly. You see, I only work for one side."

McGovern stared at him wide-eyed.

"That one," Collins stabbed a club-shaped finger in the direction of the flag. "And there are plenty like me left - enough that vermin like you should sweat with fear. We will investigate. We will arrest. We will convict. We will shame and expose. We will destroy careers and if we have to, we will take up arms. If someone subverted the electoral process by murdering my fellow citizens, I don't envy them. No, I don't envy them at all."

"Look..." whispered McGovern, cowering into his chair. " It wasn't our doing."

"Then whose?"

"No one local," stammered McGovern. "I would know. They would have to go through me. Look, anything I find out I will let you know. I just have to be real careful."

Collins nodded thoughtfully. He leaned back slowly, and the murderous look faded in his eyes after he turned and left without a word.

Back in the embassy "Reinhardt" failed to finish his dinner. The thigh wound ached somewhat, and he found himself to be a little feverish. Half-way through the afternoon he felt nauseous, but managed to force down a small amount of soup. He took a shower to rub off the day's sweat and went to bed, feeling lethargic. He found some aspirin, washed it down with alcohol from a hip flask and turned out the light.

He woke up in the darkness, feeling the cool night air on his face with relief. He threw off the blanket and let the breeze cool down his torso, but continued to sweat profusely, and his head felt heavy and sore. He threw on some clothes and went in search of the embassy doctor.

Dr Petrov was in the lounge of the compound. He was listening to the radio, gently nodding in rhythm with a Mozart symphony, another man who looked like a bodyguard staring intently at the chessboard between them. The doctor appeared to be enjoying a substantial advantage and only cast occasional glances at the board.

He interrupted the game without rancour and motioned "Reinhardt" to follow him into the medical bay. After a thorough examination the doctor diagnosed the flu. He handed out a few codeine tablets for the headache and told "Reinhardt" to sleep it off.

Marsden was where he promised to be – at the wheel of his gleaming muscle car, parked illegally and conspicuously outside a fashionable cafe. Collins shook his head in disgust, sounded his horn and motioned Marsden to follow. He drove out of the restaurant precinct and turned into a quiet street where they could speak without attracting attention.

Marsden parked behind and waited, but his instinct of hierarchy won over arrogance. He got out and got into front seat with Collins, bearing a small laptop. Collins kept his facial expression neutral. Marsden opened the computer and ran through the images.

They were shot in the Alpine foothills - that much was evident from vegetation patterns. Collins studied the picture of a small shack clad in eco-coloured iron sheeting. The trees clustered around the shack but the grass further out was closely mowed. Collins nodded for the next slide.

That was a close-up of what looked like a thick nylon line strung through a metal loop embedded in a live tree. The next shot showed the same line draped over a small zinc-coated pulley, connected to a small switching box strung up in a native bush. Another close-up showed the line tied to a small lever on the side of the box.

"That's some kind of perimeter defence," said Collins with interest.

"Right," said Marsden. "Ringed the property - must have cost a fortune."

There were totally uninspiring images taken inside the shack. What they mostly showed was a result of a savage and methodical search. The sparse furniture was upturned and slashed, and the bare wooden floor was covered with broken and displaced belongings.

Marsden touched the key, and the next shot showed a close-up of a boot print on the veranda, a familiar glue-smeared crack through the sole.

Collins sighed.

"Map," was all his said. He had to acknowledge, reluctantly, that Marsden was a much better man than his childish vanity suggested.

He leaned over and peered at the laptop, then extracted a pair of reading glasses from his jacket pocket and studied the squiggly lines with some difficulty.

"Zoom out," he ordered. Marsden reached around and touched a few keys.

"Purple Creek," said Collins. "What does a title search show?"

"Something very interesting."

"Don't piss me off," rasped Collins. "Who owns it?"

"It really is interesting. The property belongs to the Federal Attorney-General's Department."

Collins looked up from the map with a sharp intake of breath. "Why?"

"That's the other interesting thing. No records."

"How can that be?"

"Apparently, the old files were computerized in 1989. Just executive summaries, for search purposes. The original paper documents were meant to be retained for at least thirty years after the file is closed. The one in question should still be open, but they might have made a mistake and dumped it. They are always out to save space, they said."

Collins closed his eyes to get rid of Marsden's smarmy expression. He blocked out the cloying odour of Marsden's aftershave and thought frantically for a few minutes.

"All major incidents, people and file summaries were computerized from 1975," he said slowly. "I remember this from another matter. Just an executive summary, as you say, but indexed by date, name and location. You must have missed it."

"Nothing is indexed by Purple Creek. I stake my badge on it."

Collins opened his eyes.

"We just have to work harder," he replied, the reproach leaving his voice. "We need to go there."

"Now?"

Collins extracted his phone and dialled a number from memory.

"Dennis," he said urgently. "This is Jim Collins. Need a bird."

There was a long tirade on the other end.

"We won't get in their way," said Collins. "Tell

them to collect us at the hospital."

"Reinhardt" felt better as he awoke the next day. It was a hot morning, and the tiny room he was allotted was poorly served by central air conditioning. Yet he felt a light chill and pulled the blanket over his powerful shoulders as he lay still, wrestling with malaise.

The muscles felt sore as if he ran all of the previous day. Listless with fatigue, he decided to skip a daily swim. There was a little of yesterday's nausea as "Reinhardt" sipped small gulps of cold water. He remained in bed - being upright was somewhat unpleasant because of hollow-headed dizziness.

The doctor looked in on him just before lunch, checked his temperature and listened to the chest, which was largely clear. "Reinhardt" was reassured that all will be well in a few days.

###

The middle-aged triage nurse stared at them through rim-horned glasses and with undisguised alarm.

"It's not what you think, Sis," Collins reassured her with a broad grin. He splayed out his ID and waited until she read it and nodded. "There's an incoming chopper, and we are taking the return flight."

She nodded again in relief and dialled a number on the phone hanging from her neck.

"Kenny," she said briskly. "Need you down here for an escort. Two cops. Meet them at the lift."

She pointed down the corridor. "Wait at the goods lift. Big guy, red hair."

Collins and Marsden walked down the unlit corridor laden with wheelchairs, trolleys and crutches. As they approached the lift, they saw a heavy goods trolley wheeled towards them. It was easily propelled by a large, pot-bellied man in his early thirties. His hair was indeed red – as it was copious and dishevelled. The wide face bore calm, welcoming features that hospital security guards share world-over.

He checked their ID's and operated the lift with a magnetic key. Marsden helped to heave the trolley into the lift, and Collins looked at the heavy metal boxes with curiosity.

"What's all this?"

"Didn't you hear?" replied Kenny in a surprisingly high voice. "Big accident out Bairnsdale way. Bus come off the road, rolled downhill. Lots of trouble."

They both looked at him quizzically.

"They are portable fridges for organ transplants," said Kenny with a sigh. "One man's funeral, another man's christening."

Collins felt a strong desire to look away. He suppressed it.

The lift stopped inside a large glass booth perched on the roof next to the helicopter pad. Doors slid open, admitting a whistling rooftop wind that Collins found soothing on his face. He was still dressed in a suit - there was simply no time for anything else. Marsden was clearly better prepared, procuring a pair of sensible khaki pants and a stout bush shirt from his boot. His office footwear turned out to be ankle-high boots that suited his present attire equally well.

They helped Kenny push the heavy trolley from the lift and waited as the police helicopter approached the rooftop. It swung against the wind and landed with ill grace. As the machine tilted, Collins could swear that the tail rotor came close to slashing the bitumen.

Thus reassured, they wheeled the trolley towards the machine, bending down as is instinct under the whir of the blades. The door slid open, and they hefted heavy boxes into the capacious interior, where the pilot began to secure them with wide nylon straps. He gestured to the stubby seats next to the cargo and waddled towards them to help with the belt webbing.

"Hospital first," he shouted. Collins nodded.

No fuel was spared on that trip, and within an hour Collins was jolted awake as the machine landed. Marsden undid his webbing and helped manhandle the sinister load out of the helicopter. Collins registered surprise at the relief he felt from its departure.

There were excited shouts outside, and the pilot pushed Marsden towards his seat, indicating haste. They took off with what seemed to be unusual speed. As the machine swung around, Collins saw the ambulance helicopter settle on the landing pad.

After what seemed like only a few minutes of flight the pilot reduced speed and circled. He then nosed down and slowly approached the destination. After they landed he returned to the cargo bay to unbuckle their restraints.

"How long do you need?" he shouted over the noise of idling rotors. "I don't have anything on right now."

"Half-hour, max," shouted Collins. The pilot nodded and slid open the door. Collins disembarked with less than customary grace and hurried away from the blades. Marsden nimbly jumped to the ground and followed.

Away from the machine Collins straightened

his back with relief, looked around and recognized the scene from Marsden's laptop. They walked across the yellow crew-cut grass and dove under the crime scene tape that surrounded a small metal shack. Its walls were painted a dark-green hue, the only conspicuous part of the structure being the roof. It was entirely covered with solar panels that glinted in the bright sun. A nearby mast housed a satellite dish. A large water tank abutted the rear of the house in a blind corner from dusty panel windows.

The veranda of faded pine decking was empty, apart from a very old rocking chair. Collins pushed open the door and checked the floor for unwanted visitors - snakes were particularly bad that summer.

The interior was open plan - a kitchen with a log burner in one corner, a bed nearby and a long alcove which housed a Spartan sofa. The objects strewn on the floor bore no stamp of their owner's personality, being largely utilitarian in nature - a solar-powered torch, kitchen utensils, tools – apart from a few magazines. Collins extracted a pair of latex gloves from the pocket of his jacket and bent down to pick them up.

The magazines were in Cyrillic script. Each was clearly retained for a specific reason, the relevant pages marked with yellow adhesive notes. The writing on the notes was in elegant longhand, which Collins could not read.

"We'll take them," he said to Marsden. The younger man accepted the bundle.

There was a small shelf opposite the sofa, and the wires hanging over its edge suggested that it used to house a computer. The bottom of the shelf was entirely occupied with a stack of car batteries, clearly intended for the same computer. A disconnected satellite transceiver forlornly perched on the floor nearby.

Collins studied the scene with care and lifted the sofa, tipping it on the side with one hand. The bottom was slashed and clearly searched with some care. He turned away and kept studying the surroundings. Marsden waited in silence.

After some minutes of contemplation Collins approached the shelf and began to lift the batteries one by one. On the third try he exclaimed and pulled the battery off the shelf.

Marsden let out a whispered exclamation as Collins turned it over and worked a small latch on its black casing. The bottom swung away from the rest of the box, and a spool of discs wrapped in a plastic bag tumbled onto the floor.

Totally unperturbed, as if collecting change after buying a newspaper, Collins unwrapped the plastic bag and studied the top disc in the spool. It was marked with felt pen in the same foreign longhand. He wrapped up the plastic and handed it back to Marsden.

"We'll take those too," he said absently.

Marsden followed him outside, where Collins already extracted his phone. But after a moment he glanced at the set and frowned.

"No reception," he said with annoyance and started walking towards the helicopter.

Marsden spent a little time trying to shut the broken front door. By the time he turned around, Collins was engaged in an animated conversation with the pilot. The latter was gesturing and shaking his head.

Finally, Collins turned away, patted the pilot on the shoulder in a conciliatory gesture and walked back towards Marsden.

"Go with him to Melbourne," he said shortly.

"What about you?"

"Local airport, then Canberra."

Marsden nodded his understanding.

The machine rose above the treetops and gathered speed towards the low afternoon sun. Collins stared down at the dry landscape with a kind of hunger that comes from leaving behind unrealized hopes. Suddenly he unbuckled the restraints and clambered forward towards the cockpit.

The pilot stared at him with what must have been anger, but Collins emphatically stabbed downwards with his finger. The pilot turned away with an angry jerk of the helmeted head and pointed the machine towards the ground.

They landed on another faded paddock in what must have been the next valley. Collins slid open the door and ran towards a rundown farmhouse some distance away. Marsden waited, then freed himself from the webbing with a short curse and followed.

An elderly woman in a rumpled black dress was chopping wood next to the house. Marsden was amazed to see that her casual strokes split the heavy logs as if they were matchsticks.

She saw the helicopter but took its appearance in her stride. As Collins approached, she sank the gleaming blade into the chopping block and turned towards them. Her brown features were creased in a frown, and she removed the cigarette that glowed in the corner of her mouth. She waited for them to approach, strands of long grey hair hanging over her broad forehead, ruffled by the breeze from the helicopter.

"Mother," said Collins respectfully. "I am with police."

She nodded. "Have ya found 'im?"

"Do you mean Mr Meister?"

"No, Father Christmas," she chided. "Do yews know what happened or not?"

"Not as yet," said Collins. "I need to know something that you can probably tell me. What is the name of this place?"

"Purple Creek, they call it now."

"But what was it called before?"

The old woman chuckled wryly.

"Blackie's Creek," she told him. "They changed it, ooh, twenty-year ago. Some white poofta decided it was racist, see! An' it wasn't, ya know - it was about them black cockatoos. Beautiful, they are. Sing so sad."

Collins chuckled to show his appreciation of the irony.

"Did... Do you know him well?" he asked.

"Neh. Kept to 'imself, funny man. Saw him drive past sometimes. Always waved back. We never got to yack or nothing. But neighbour is neighbour. When me grandson heard them shots, he drove to town and called the coppers, good and proper."

Collins stared for a second.

"Thank you, Mother," he told her and turned, beckoning Marsden to follow. They boarded the helicopter and rode to the airport in silence.

"Reinhardt" awoke at dusk to realize that he is sicker than ever, and for the first time in his life he felt a genuine fear of losing control over his steel-limbed body. Many years ago a bullet pierced his shoulder in a training accident, and he was hospitalized with a wound infection. He felt much worse now, he realized. He sought out the doctor and asked to be checked again.

Responding to the obvious concern, the doctor was even more thorough. He sat down and carefully recorded all of the man's recent travels, his medical history and habits. He noted that like all FSB assassins, the patient was in perfect health, not even a casual smoker, a rare drinker who maintained his super-fit physique with a punishing regime of daily exercise. During a long examination the assassin was checked from the top of his close-cropped skull to his toes, scarred by thousands of kilometres he marched and ran in heavy boots. But apart from fever, the obvious clamminess of his skin and some redness in the throat, nothing unusual was found.

Just to be on the safe side, the doctor

administered a shot of penicillin and sent "Reinhardt" back to bed.

"As promised, my love."

Raisa smiled at him languidly, stepping out of the shower. She took his hand for balance and pressed against the towel Klimov extended around her shoulders.

He inhaled the smell of fresh soap as he pressed his mouth into the back of her neck. It was a good afternoon, spent in gentle lovemaking after a long sleep. He brushed away his anxiety about a mission that suddenly morphed from a simple, obvious operation into a nightmare with many uncertainties. But that was anything new, and there were many backups in place.

Klimov had prioritized these on the drive back to Canberra. Early morning saw phone calls placed to a contact in Victorian emergency services, once a firebrand socialist who was now busy organizing an exercise in the foothills.

According to the scenario, a man with a mental illness has driven into the bush and set off on foot across rough terrain. Poorly equipped, he wasn't expected to survive for more than a few days unless apprehended. Klimov chuckled - whatever plan Morozov made, it was unlikely to include helicopters with thermal imaging.

The next call was to a high-flying forensic accountant, a child of two fervent Communists who escaped from Germany just before the war. He was now busy with Morozov's banking profile. Within a day or so Klimov expected to know all transactions pertaining to Morozov's life for the past twelve months. Credit card monitoring is a handy way to find missing persons, no matter how much they wish to remain missing.

A further perusal of Klimov's notes dredged up another upright citizen, who once upon a time was lured into the Trotskyist society of a second-rate university. The gangly, acne-riddled youth was one of the few virgins on campus, but fiery ladies and more than a few gentlemen, allegedly devoted to the cause of military communism, righted that wrong with gusto; Trotsky would have applauded with mirth. For some years studies and even the cause of world revolution were much less on the boy's talented mind than marijuana and romps on soiled mattresses. But talent won out in the end, and the studies were crowned with success. Unlike the world revolution, thought Klimov wryly.

Decades had passed, and the amply deflowered young man was now a seasoned expert in telecommunications. In deference to the residue of his youthful beliefs, he spurned the advances of Silicon Valley, remaining a boffin at the local telephone monopoly. In due course it was privatized and devolved into the wolf pack of big business, but the man was too set in his ways to seek a socially responsible employer.

More to the point, however, the former Trotskyist was instantly able to tap into the giant mainframe that monitored cell phone traffic. His orders were to pinpoint Morozov's number if possible - if not, to look for the appropriate pattern in the relevant district and monitor all possible matches until coincidences began to accrue.

Sooner or later - hopefully, sooner - one of these efforts would bear fruit. Klimov decided to trust in that thought as he dressed into a neat pair of dark-blue pants and a white shirt, ironed to perfection. The intelligence gathering might have seen better days, but there was nothing wrong with the embassy's laundry.

Raisa emerged from the bathroom looking resplendent. Dark hair framed the neat oval of her face. She wore pants of light beige cotton, with a white blouse to offset her trim figure. There was a single string of amber around her neck with modest matching earrings. Klimov's pulse quickened in adoration and fear.

They walked down to the lobby of the compound and found the duty officer, a young man with startling blue eyes and a mop of dirty-blonde hair.

The duty officer jumped to his feet and drew himself to attention. Klimov ran his eyes over a trim figure, and his probing gaze returned to the head. New times permitted the hair to be long enough to show a hint of spike. That would serve him very poorly in a fight, Klimov sighed inwardly.

"We are going out to Rosalie's for dinner," he told the young man. "Could you lend us the most decadent limousine on offer?"

"With pleasure, Comrade Colonel," the young man rummaged in a drawer of his desk. "The very best there is."

Their steed turned out to be a midnight-blue BMW saloon, a large muscle car of some age but in perfect condition. Klimov opened the door for Raisa, who blew him a mock glamour kiss as she climbed inside.

The steel gates topped by razor wire rattled open, and Klimov pulled out without bothering with his seat belt - their favourite Italian restaurant was only a few suburbs away. Even notorious parking problems failed to get in the way of a perfect evening, as he deftly reversed into a spot a few metres from Rosalie's.

They chose a table on the footpath. Sipping the first offerings of cold Sauvignon Blanc, they were sheltered from the heat of setting sun by a thick pastel umbrella.

Klimov felt as he hadn't felt for a long time - two normal human beings celebrating their mature age. He placed his hand over Raisa's as they studied the menus. She turned and smiled at him radiantly.

"What a perfect evening," she said gently.

The small plane already waited for them on the landing strip. No time was wasted - Collins was already strapping himself into the co-pilot's seat as the police helicopter rose overhead.

The pilot of the plane was an older man with handlebar moustache, who looked like he made a sparse living out of spreading chemicals over dry paddocks. He was disinclined to ask questions, and Collins stared out of the window as the nimble machine ate up the distance to Canberra. Collins checked his watch: he hoped to arrive before sunset.

They shunned the main airport, landing in a small private strip just outside the city. Collins emerged from the cockpit, watching the police cruiser race towards them. He raised his hand in thanks to the pilot and boarded the cruiser, which began moving as soon as he was in his seat. By the time he shut the door and began to pull at his seat belt, the cruiser was already out of the gate and accelerating down a dusty road. The young driver appeared completely immersed in the task.

Collins extracted his phone and checked the screen. Marsden has already been in touch. Collins redialled the number.

"Russian," gasped Marsden into the phone. "Sorry, I was just doing a few press-ups between jobs."

"What?" asked Collins irritably.

"The magazines and the DVD's are in Russian. The films appear to be a collection of recent Russian telemovies. You know - thrillers, soaps, historical drama. That kind of stuff. But the magazines are a little more interesting."

Collins waited, not wasting further energy on prompts.

"All the marked articles refer to the present political crisis in Russia," he heard Marsden's voice. "A few references to the war in the Caucasus had been heavily underlined. Do you need anything more specific?"

"That will do for now," said Collins. "Except I forgot to ask - where was the boot print found?"

"All around," replied Marsden. "They said that all men in what we think were the raiding party wore the same kind of boot. It definitely wasn't the shack's tenant - we found his footwear at the shack, and it's two sizes larger than the glued boot."

"Thanks," said Collins, already shutting off the phone. He then paused and thought, but finally replaced the unit in his pocket. It was sometimes better to arrive unannounced.

They sped through Canberra and past the grassy hill of Parliament. The cruiser swung into the car park of a very modern building, whose façade of tinted glass overlooked the lake. Collins told the driver to wait and marched towards the faceted entrance.

"Reinhardt" awoke in the dark, feeling dizzy with fever. After taking a deep breath he began to convulse in a fit of coughing.

Searing pain flooded his chest. He gasped and rolled out of bed, doubling up on the carpet with an agonising moan, a stream of sharp icicles racing inside his airways. With what seemed like the last of his strength he hammered on the thin wooden door, trying to hold his breath.

His air ran out, he let go. An explosive exhalation sprayed blood-stained mucus across the wall. Then he passed out.

###

Ludenko finished coding the message and gave it to the officer in the radio room. As he lit a cigarette and stared into the night sky from the roof garden, the microwave signal streamed over the low hills surrounding Canberra towards a far-away satellite, which bounced the message to a station in the Pamir Mountains, from where it was redirected to the other side of the globe.

"Your Excellency!"

He turned around to see the doctor standing at the door. He immediately dropped his cigarette and crushed it out - not because of guilt about his habit, but because the doctor was an experienced man with many years of embassy work, a veteran of many crises that had to be solved with little more than kitchen utensils. Such a man was not rattled easily - but panic was all over his face.

The doctor explained the situation in a few terse sentences, their clarity and brevity evidence to his experience in having to involve powerful laymen in medical decisions.

Secrecy often required that urgent treatment was forgone in favour of a hasty return home. Sometimes the patient died in a curtained-off area behind the cockpit while other passengers ate lunch and drank champagne in the next row of seats.

"As a guess, what is it?" asked Ludenko. The soldier's presence was technically illegal, but if hospital treatment was required, a legal entry into the country could be faked easily enough.

It didn't sound as if the patient was in any condition to discuss his profession, and there was no possible scandal attached to him falling ill, whatever the devil was the problem. That more or less circumscribed the ambassador's concerns, sentimentality being a luxury he was taught to go without.

"I can't hazard a better guess than a tropical illness, and whatever it is, it's a vicious thing. He has a bad fever and a blood-stained cough. That's all I can tell you without tests, and I can only pray it is not very infectious."

Ludenko stared at the doctor with resentment.

"Have him hospitalized. Single room, full sedation if possible. Stay with him and make sure he doesn't babble once he wakes up. Notify me of his condition every four hours."

The doctor left, and Ludenko returned to the balcony, staying out of bright moonlight by sheer habit. It wasn't until he extracted another cigarette and brought it near the mouth that the thought struck home. He tried to return the cigarette to the packet, but it bent, and he tossed it over the guard rail in annoyance.

As ordered, the doctor quickly arranged an admission to a private room in Canberra Hospital. It was instantly turned into an intensive care bed, as "Reinhardt" deteriorated with speed that was beyond all imagination of his attendants.

It was soon apparent that he was dying, despite being ventilated and pumped full of antibiotics. He arrived to hospital in a coma, his circulation on the edge of collapse. An infusion of stimulants barely managed to stabilize his blood pressure at a level necessary for survival.

Petrov conferred with the registrar outside the room. Through the small window he could see that the soldier posed no risk to security - he was deeply unconscious, mouth fully occupied by a ventilation tube. The clear plastic of the tube was stained with pink foam from inside. A catheter draining the bladder was connected to a bag, quarter-full with dark-red fluid.

A monitor above the bed showed the heart tracing, oxygen saturation and blood pressure. They all looked ominous. Blood pressure was very low, and the heart rhythm was a thready cadence, interrupted by extraneous beats. The patient was clearly at death's door.

"Any ideas?" asked Petrov.

"Viraemia of some kind. We have his travel

history, but that doesn't help us. Are you sure there is nothing else we should know?" the registrar wiped his hands with a paper towel and looked at Petrov with hostility. He was a tall, blond youth with a South African accent - Petrov was left in no doubt that he was in enemy territory.

"Such as?"

"Such as why does an embassy clerk have such a fit, scarred body? And what the devil is this?"

The tall Aryan turned to the keyboard and punched a few keys. A crisp X-Ray image appeared on the screen, and Petrov recognised that he was looking at the right thigh. Buried in the flesh of the quadriceps was a metal object.

"Is this actually in the leg?" asked Petrov.

"Yes, here's a lateral." The registrar moved the mouse, bringing up a film taken from another angle. It confirmed that the object was indeed deep inside the thigh, rather than on its surface.

A few clicks magnified the image to fill the screen. It looked like a dart with a small attachment on the tail, which appeared to be less dense - possibly a tiny glass ampoule that shattered inside the thigh.

"I don't know what that is," said Petrov angrily. Klimov had some explaining to do. "But I will go and ask questions immediately."

He stormed off into the corridor and called the embassy, asking for Klimov.

Uniformed security guards were clearly perturbed by his appearance. He held up his ID, which was taken from him somewhat rudely, but returned with deference.

"I need to see the duty officer," said Collins.

After a brief call the security men gestured towards the white metal archway. Collins gritted his teeth - he hated metal detectors. Over the years he developed a phobia of these shrill devices, having been stopped in the middle of urgent tasks by pens, loose coins, metal in the soles of combat boots - let alone weapons that he had the right to carry into secure areas.

He evolved a routine to minimize this outrage - all metal objects were housed in the jacket pockets. The belt buckle was heavy plastic, with a face that resembled dark metal.

He tossed the jacket into the proffered basket and strode past the gate. The machine had the grace to remain silent; Collins collected his jacket and turned to the guards.

He was escorted towards the lift and led down the plush corridor clad in new-smelling carpet of electric blue, already faded from the burning sunlight that poured through the glass wall.

The duty officer was a thin-shouldered man in his early forties, his pleasant face brimmed with dark curly hair. He was clad in a neat white suit with a knitted brown tie. The combination didn't quite work, decided Collins.

He checked the name on the ID: Charles Deakin. An illustrious dynasty - Collins bumped into a few descendants of the great man. They were all quiet and formidable achievers.

"Your department's predecessor purchased land and built a small house in a cosy little valley in Victoria, at what was then called Blackie's Creek," he said without a preamble. "I need to find out why and when. There will be no memos, delays or paperwork, Mr Deakin. I am working on the strike murders, and you know who I am."

"I'll only ask for a requisition order under your signature," replied Deakin. "You can write it on my letterhead right now, sign it and endorse it with your badge number. I will get to work right away."

Collins nodded his thanks and slid the proffered paper and pen towards him. He checked the date and time on his watch, then began to scrawl.

Deakin turned away from his desk, adorned by a neat laptop nestled into a docking station. To the left and behind was a small shelf which housed an old-fashioned terminal with an inbuilt keyboard. He turned it on and began to type his login details.

Collins finished off his opus with a broad signature. Deakin briefly stared across his desk to read it, nodded and returned to the terminal. The screen was invisible to Collins, and he monitored the proceedings by Deakin's facial expression.

Which did not look promising.

"Top secret," said Deakin with genuine chagrin. "I will have to fill out an incident report just because I tried to access it. Bugger."

"Can you read it?" asked Collins curtly.

"Of course not," replied Deakin irritably. "You need authorization to even think about reading it."

"Get me the boss."

"Which one?"

Collins pointed upstairs. "No chain-of-command crap, young man. Straight to the roof

- I am very pressed for time."

Deakin thought furiously for a few seconds. He then turned away to log himself off, shut down the terminal and stood up, requisition request in hand.

"Come with me," he said curtly.

"Panic-monger," said Raisa accusingly. She drank the last of her wine and sat back contently. It was cooler now that it got dark, terracotta tiles giving up the last of the day's heat.

Klimov bent across the table to rest his lips over her forehead briefly.

"Guilty," he said happily. His eyes filled with moisture that flowed into Raisa's hair.

She bent towards him and ran a soft hand over his forearm.

"Just one blockage," she said apologetically. "My brother had four."

"Well, it's all done," Klimov told her. "The new cholesterol pills will take care of the rest. I told you they know what they are doing. But remember what they said - you need to take it very quietly for the next few months."

###

They rode the lift to the top floor, walked down another blue corridor and entered a large antechamber that was all glass. Collins was instantly grateful that it wasn't the middle of the day - even in late summer the sun would be unbearable.

In the middle of the antechamber stood a long mahogany desk. Its surface could pass for a bar in a modest ski lodge, and most of it was pristinely empty. An ageing woman in a severe dark suit sat behind the desk and stared at some document with disdain.

Deakin approached the desk with what looked like supplication and placed the requisition on the edge of the desk. The woman's carefully plucked brows rose with disgust at the scrawled handwriting.

Collins gave her a few seconds to read what he wrote, then he approached the desk and thrust his ID into her hand. He jerked his head in a curt gesture towards the large set of doors behind the desk.

She stared at him contemptuously, and Collins allowed his expression to harden. She hurriedly lifted a small black phone from the cradle, dialling a number by touch.

"My apologies, Dr Stockley," she said in a surprisingly melodious voice. "An important man has come to see you on some urgent business. Very well, thank you."

She replaced the unit and looked at Collins with acidic defiance. He merely reached forward to sweep the ID and the requisition from the desk.

Stockley emerged from the double doors, clad in his usual resplendence - a shirt that glowed white under a mauve-and-grey silk tie secured with a gold pin. He wore perfectly pressed grey trousers, and his dark pumps shone like mirrors.

He ushered the men into his office, reading the requisition as he walked.

"An unexpected pleasure, I am sure," he gave Collins a thin smile, his eyes two chunks of grey ice. He eyed the rumpled clothes anointed by Gippsland dust with curiosity that was almost anthropological. "But Mr Deakin is entirely correct - entries with that classification cannot be accessed without going through proper channels."

"I could call Arnold," replied Collins. "I could make the trip to the other lake, talk to him, and he would call you. I would then come back, and you would show me the file. Then again, I could just charge you with obstruction and make an arrest. In fact, that way I only have to make one trip."

Stockley stared in consternation, well aware

that he was caught in a gap between regulations and conventions. His department had no real mandate to conceal information from an inquiry into multiple murders, and the media aspect was rather threatening as well.

Stockley shook his head to clear the latter spectre from his mind and stared at Collins for a brief moment.

"I've made a decision," he announced, nodding to Deakin. "Do it."

He led them to a large rolltop desk at the corner of his office and sprung open the lid. It contained another terminal like Deakin's.

"You fop," thought Collins. "The mainframe terminal is too old-fashioned for your décor, so you had a whole bloody desk made around it. My taxes at work."

Deakin manipulated the keys, then stood back deferentially. Stockley sat down at the terminal like a piano teacher demonstrating to a slow pupil, elegantly lowered his hands to the keyboard and typed in his code. He then stood up and stared at Collins, as if expecting applause.

Deakin resumed control of his keyboard. His face first lit up as he located the file, but sank as he saw the contents.

"Corrupted," he said in a flat voice.

Moving with speed that even surprised himself, Collins pushed past Stockley, circumnavigated the desk and came around to lean over Deakin's shoulder. He stared at the screen in violation of numerous commandments, but all he saw was gibberish – nothing more than a short string of random characters. It did not even look like cypher, and it was mercilessly short – a mere two lines, most of the characters being asterisks. Even if encrypted, it did not look like it could contain useful information.

"It's a very old file," said Stockley with what Collins perceived as a trace of glee. "When they are not updated on the system, we often lose them. That's technology for you."

Collins looked at them in fury.

"It's true, Assistant Commissioner," said Deakin. "We get this all the time - they gave us money for this lovely new building but refused to update the mainframe. A lot of old records are now going missing."

"We will check personnel records and speak to anyone who may have been involved in this operation, retired or not," said Stockley. "Provided, of course, that they are still alive."

"That's the next step," agreed Collins.

"It will, I am afraid, take some time."

"I can only thank you for cooperation, Director-General," replied Collins formally, allowing a trace of sarcasm to creep into his voice. "I don't wish to take any more of your precious time."

He rode the lift back to the lobby, where Deakin handed him over to security guards, preventing the lift doors from closing with one hand. Collins nodded, and Deakin stepped back inside the lift. He noticed that the guards stared at him with alarm but chose to ignore it.

But when he stepped out into the car park, his instincts began to cry foul. The expanse of bitumen was empty apart from one security van and the police cruiser. The driver stood beside his car in a bulletproof vest.

"What's going on?" asked Collins shortly.

"No one knows just yet," replied the young constable. "They declared a state of emergency."

"Territory or nationwide?"

"Both."

"Any other information?"

"Not on our channel. All off-duty personnel were told to report in. They are going to close all roads shortly. We have to return to HQ."

###

"I understand, Your Excellency," said Klimov deferentially. "I propose that we return as planned, without drawing attention. Yes, thirty minutes at the most. Of course, Your Excellency. As discussed."

He stared into the dead phone with contempt and returned it to his shirt pocket.

"What an oaf," he told Raisa lightly.

"Is something wrong?"

"Yes, a bit of a setback," sighed Klimov, raising the dessert menu from his table. "Not entirely anticipated, I have to confess, but it will be dealt with, all the same."

She winced, rubbing her left breast.

"What's that?" asked Klimov shortly, sitting up.

"No, it's not heart," she told him, moving back and forth experimentally. "I think it's the way I was positioned during the procedure - it's been hurting ever since, and I moved awkwardly just now."

"Are you sure you don't need the spray?"

"No, no," she smiled. "It's different. What are

you having for dessert?"

He returned to the menu.

"It would have to be tiramisu," he told her. "Maybe you should indulge as well, now that we are on top of the problem."

"No," she replied with disapproval. "I mustn't get a taste for such things ever again. The fruit salad with Cointreau will be perfectly suitable."

Klimov looked up to summon the waitress, and his senses went on alert that instant. The plump young woman was speaking to an older couple seated inside the restaurant. She motioned towards the counter surrounded with customers, credit cards in hand.

The couple hastily downed the remains of their coffee, rose and joined the melee at the counter.

The waitress walked across to the next table, where the pantomime was repeated in much the same manner.

Klimov turned around and noted that many people were on the street, walking towards their cars with what appeared to be some haste. In fact, there were now many empty spots along the curved street that was jammed with cars only minutes before.

The waitress walked out of the restaurant

and bent down to their table, revealing a glistening cleavage.

"Very sorry, sir," she told Klimov, radiating cheap perfume. "You have to evacuate."

"What?" gasped Raisa. "Here?"

Klimov held up an admonishing hand.

"What's happening?" he demanded in a curt officer's voice.

"We received instructions via the emergency response system," she told him. "Everyone has to return to their homes immediately and stay inside. At ten pm all roads will be closed. That's all I know, sorry."

"But that's... martial law!" whispered Raisa. She reached for the red spray bottle, beads of sweat appearing on her forehead. "Valera... What is going on?"

Klimov studied the message on his cell phone. It was beamed to all handsets in the region, it appeared, and it said much the same as the young heifer.

"We will know soon enough," he told her through gritted teeth. He handed the waitress three crisp bills and waved off the offer of change. She left, mouthing indistinct thanks.

Raisa was ill - Klimov realized that, watching

her during the short walk to the car. She was a little breathless, and her gait was no longer a sure swivel of lean hips. As he held open the door and studied her face intently, she made no attempt to reassure him.

He drove back to the embassy and escorted her to their suite. She fell onto the bed, clutching her spray bottle.

"I have to speak to Ludenko," he told her. "Will you be all right?"

She waved him off. "Don't be long."

Klimov ran down the stairs and crossed the concrete yard in a few leaps. Ludenko awaited him in a gloomy office adorned with pseudo-antique furniture and recently changed portraits.

"What can you tell me about your wet business?" asked Ludenko without a preamble. "Wet work" was the old KGB term for assassination.

Klimov held his breath. Compartmentalization of the mission was never discussed with Lebedev, he realized now. There was too much haste on departure.

Ludenko studied his face, making an educated guess about Klimov's thoughts.

"Let me tell you why I ask," he said coldly.

"Your cut-throat has just died of some kind of exotic infection in hospital. I need to know whether what he had was contagious. I do have responsibility for every living soul in the compound."

Klimov nodded, feeling a spasm in his throat.

"Very well, Your Excellency," he said hoarsely. A decision of his career has just been made, and there was no going back. "I will explain what I know."

Ten minutes later he ran back to his room, where Raisa was sitting up in bed. She looked a little better and quite composed.

"We are going," Klimov told her simply. He stretched out his hand, and she rose to follow. They walked back downstairs and confronted the duty officer.

"I have to get her out," said Klimov simply, holding Raisa's hand in a stronger grip than he realized.

The duty officer hesitated.

"Keys," ordered Klimov, a note of steel ringing in his voice. He stared at the young man intently, watching for signs of disobedience. He was unsure whether the embassy staff were armed in unprecedented circumstances, and it was clear that all the usual bets were off.

After a moment's hesitation the duty officer returned the keys and slid across a form, which Klimov signed without looking. They stared at each other for a few more seconds, then Klimov nodded and turned to Raisa.

Her colour is getting worse, whispered a little demon inside him. Three hours to Sydney, replied Klimov. It will work out.

They returned to the vehicle, and he lifted Raisa inside - she folded her legs into the passenger well obediently and limply. Klimov fastened her seat belt and leaned across the seat to kiss her. There was a sweaty coldness to her skin, but her eyes shone bright from his kiss.

"We will be there in no time," said Klimov tenderly. She nodded and closed her eyes.

He reversed out of the car park and drove up to the gate, his hand on the pistol at his waistline. If anything was going to happen - it would be now, with the vehicle trapped against solid metal.

The gate slid open.

Klimov resisted the urge to gun the engine and gently guided the vehicle over the bumpy exit, turning into the street. Only then did he depress the accelerator and gathered speed.

There was no traffic, he noted, and the restaurant precinct was empty. He sped through deserted streets, ignoring stop signs and traffic lights, turning into a back road that skirted around a secret facility. Secret, he noted in passing, for anyone but his department.

The back road was completely empty, and Klimov allowed the large BMW its head. Powerful lights bounced over the road, and he just managed to slow down for a concrete ford, now nearly dry.

The vehicle bounced heavily over the concrete bottom of the ford and slid slightly on the slimy residue of the waterway. Klimov ground his teeth in annoyance and gunned the accelerator again. Gathering speed, he looked at Raisa - she opened her eyes when the car bounced, then closed them again, seeming content.

"Valera," she said weakly but steadily.

"My love."

"Who has done this?"

"Someone who used to work for us," he replied tersely. "I was sent here to stop it."

"Mother of God, Valera," she sighed, shaking her head weakly. "Promise me something."

He nodded, staring ahead at the dark road. Within minutes he took a wide bend and was turning into the Federal Highway, letting the engine absorb some of the speed over the cloverleaf entry. Once back on the highway, he set the cruise control at just above the speed limit and sat back in the seat. Canberra and its horrors were behind them.

"Make sure you put it right," said Raisa.

Klimov nodded curtly and scanned the instrument panel for the first time. The vehicle was fully fuelled, other gauges seeming to indicate that all was well. Raisa rested peacefully, and he began to formulate the remainder of the plan - he decided to ring the Russian consulate in Sydney and have a hospital bed ready.

He finished his thought as another part of his conscience scrambled his foot to brake. The vehicle lurched as Klimov brought down the speed in order to approach the checkpoint in what may pass for a leisurely manner.

The checkpoint reminded Klimov how much he underestimated these people. Three policemen, acting with no warning and no allocated resources, blocked the highway with a monstrous bulldozer from the road works he passed a few kilometres ago. They were well-armed with army-issue Steyr assault rifles in addition to their side arms. All three wore bulletproof vests and riot helmets with shields, which were probably as good a defence against infection as anything available at short notice.

Two men positioned themselves on the roof of the bulldozer's cabin, training their rifles at the approaching vehicle. The third took his chances on the ground, his rifle butt held against the shoulder, paratrooper-fashion. He clearly thought it out, taking care not to stand between the car and the other rifles.

Klimov drove up to him and slid down the window, sizing up his adversary - ageing, powerful frame, drooping moustache on a wide face behind the Lexan shield. The relaxed way in which he held the rifle indicated maturity and experience, something Klimov immediately took on board.

"Accredited diplomat," he said calmly. "I need to pass."

"Impossible, sir," replied the policeman. "No one goes in or out."

"But you cannot obstruct me," argued Klimov, waving his diplomatic passport in the man's face. "That contravenes the Geneva Convention on diplomatic protection."

"With respect, sir," came the reply. "What you just said is a complete load of rubbish. Diplomats do not have automatic laissez-passer other than to embassy grounds. I've done twenty years in the protective service."

"She has a heart problem," shouted Klimov, throwing his passport into the back seat. "You know I cannot take her to the hospitals in Canberra."

"I am very sorry," said the policeman, staring at Raisa intently. "But I won't be letting anyone out. Most of my family is in Sydney, so even if they changed my orders, I would not obey them."

Klimov froze to check an involuntary movement as his hand twitched down towards his waist and the concealed pistol. The bulldozer covered both lanes of the road, leaving a very unlikely amount of space - the likelihood of getting through a tricky turn without having most of the vehicle shot away from under him was negligible.

He could drive away and double-back through the bushes on foot - he had no doubt that he could take out three men under the cover of darkness. But the straight road went a long way - he would have to drive more than a kilometre before being able to conceal his intentions, and then he would have to cover the same distance on foot in dress shoes. It would take half the night.

Out of evident options, Klimov stared at the obstacle helplessly.

"Hey," said the obstacle with sudden urgency. "Your lady doesn't look too good."

Klimov whipped his head to the left and gasped in horror. Raisa has slumped down, seat belt obscuring her face. Klimov touched her neck - it was ice-cold, clammy, with a thready pulse that felt irregular and fast. She did not respond.

"I will radio for an ambulance to meet you if they can," yelled the policeman, running beside him as Klimov began to reverse.

He nodded and quickly accelerated away from the road block. The rest of the manoeuvre was distinctly undiplomatic, with the vehicle executing a perfect handbrake turn and roaring, tyres squealing and smoking, towards the distant city. Klimov reached a very high speed and prohibited himself to look at Raisa.

His trained mind weighed up the options - her only chance of survival lay in receiving help, and all he could do was get her there, as fast as his skills allowed.

He ran the first traffic lights on the way back, then slowed down to legal speed, seeing red and blue lights flash ahead. As they came closer he was impressed to see that the cop he was willing to shoot in cold blood kept his word - two ambulances, lights rotating slowly, were parked at the roadside in front of another roadblock, this one set up in a more professional fashion with movable barriers.

Klimov flashed his lights, and one of the ambulances flashed back an acknowledgement. Only then did he permit himself to look sideways - Raisa was still slumped in the same posture, her jaw now slack and eyes wide open.

The remainder was a blur that began with Klimov braking hard and skidding across the road to bring the vehicle to a stop just opposite the ambulance doors. Four burly men ran towards the car and wrenched open Raisa's door. They hefted her limp body onto the trolley and raced back to the ambulance.

Klimov stared, and his mind barely registered that her white blouse was torn open, paddles were pressed against ghostly white flesh, and her torso jerked in response. By the very bright headlights of his car he saw tanned, muscular arms pumping the glistening chest, someone frantically sliding a tube into her mouth. He sat still, grasping the sweaty steering wheel, as he saw the paddles come down again. There was another jolt, then one more. He could not tell how long it continued.

When the men stepped away from the trolley and covered what was left of his lifetime companion with a white sheet, Klimov's frantic eyes opened wide and lost all focus.

One of the ambulance officers approached

and opened the driver's door, kneeling next to the car on the ground. The face behind a protective shield was covered in grime, tears welling up in bright, young eyes.

"I am very sorry," he told Klimov hoarsely. "We did everything we could."

Klimov remained still, letting the horror absorb him fully. The mean little voice of doom fell silent inside him, its job now done.

With guilt, Klimov registered relief - there was nothing left to fear, and there was nothing left to lose. His worst nightmare turned into reality, and it was a liberation.

The ambulance officer put his large hand on Klimov's shoulder, and they sat together, not moving. After a while Klimov reached up and squeezed the sweaty hand in silent thanks.

"We will take her to the hospital, sir," said the second paramedic. "Things are a bit tight there at the moment, and you will need to give them a while before calling them. Can I have some details?"

Klimov nodded curtly, his mind forcing itself back into focus. He handed over Raisa's passport and looked away as the trolley was loaded into the ambulance.

"Address is care of the Russian embassy," he added tonelessly.

As he looked up to receive the returned document, he saw that the ambulance doors were now shut. The young officer ran towards the cabin and jumped in.

The big vehicle turned around and drove away, its emergency lights now off. Klimov started the engine and followed, the armed men at the checkpoint making no effort to stop him. He drove along the empty street, tail lights of the ambulance receding ahead in the distance. They slid into a roundabout and disappeared behind tall shrubbery – the final glimpse of everything that was good and reassuring in Klimov's world dissolved into darkness.

He settled into void, drifting along in a timeless, thoughtless state until he found himself at the gates of the embassy. The security camera swivelled and metal grated open with an irritating squeal. Klimov drove up to the door of the service building and got out of the car, barely remembering to switch off the engine.

He walked inside, holding Raisa's handbag next to the chest. The guard immediately registered Klimov's crumpled, tear-streaked face and stood at attention as Klimov approached.

"Your orders, Comrade Colonel," he said in a brisk, polite voice.

"She is dead..." whispered Klimov, his eyes welling up with fresh tears.

The young man's composure tightened, and he shook the dishevelled blonde head in a gesture of genuine distress.

"I am very sorry, Comrade Colonel," he replied sincerely. "Anything I can do - just say."

Klimov nodded his appreciation and held up his palm in a gesture of pause as he thought briefly.

"Take this," he told the duty officer, handing over Raisa's bag. "She wished to be cremated, which is what they are likely to do at the hospital anyway. Please send someone down there to ensure that her remains are repatriated and released to her family in Moscow. All details are on file."

"It will be a privilege, Comrade Colonel."

"Thank you. I now need to do a few things."

Klimov walked past the reception and keyed in his code at the office door. For the next twenty minutes he systematically gathered what he required, stowing the documents in a plastic bag. Satisfied that he had what he wanted, he slid the bag under his shirt and restored his clothing to a respectable state.

He walked back out to reception, where the young man was barking hurried orders into a portable radio. Seeing Klimov, he ordered his respondent to wait and stared expectantly.

"Tell the others that I had reactivated the mission," said Klimov. "The survivors are to stay put and await further developments."

"Certainly, Comrade Colonel. Anything else?"

Klimov stopped and thought for a brief moment, aware that he may be speaking his mother tongue for the last time.

"Tell my in-laws not to wait for me when they organize the funeral," he said tonelessly. "I am unlikely to survive."

Klimov felt the young man's stare at his back as he walked out through the sliding doors. He got into the car, started the engine and reversed it to the gate, which slid open obediently. The wheels bounced over the uneven pavement, and he turned into the empty traffic lane.

This time nothing held him back, and he floored the accelerator as soon as the forward gear had engaged.

###

Collins wiped his forehead for the third time since the briefing began. The paper napkin in his hand was now soaked, and he crumpled it in his fist.

"The Russian Embassy," he said to no one in particular.

Heads swivelled towards him, and Arnold returned from the balcony door, the unlit cigarette hanging limply from the corner of his mouth.

"Your meaning, Assistant Commissioner?" he asked avidly.

Collins shook his head, thinking frantically.

"Don't quite have one," he rumbled after a few seconds' delay. "Just sorting out my thoughts."

Arnold nodded and walked out onto the balcony. He lit the cigarette and leaned on the rails with his back, staring into the room full of senior officers.

"To summarize so far," he told them. "Russian Embassy clerk, looks too fit to be a clerk, dies after two days of being unwell. Cause unknown, but presumed infectious. Numerous hospital and embassy personnel are exposed and had plenty of time to pass the presumed infection to many others. Ideas, anyone? Connections with current cases?"

"It's a very long shot," said Collins. He lifted

the phone and dialled Marsden's number. "But here goes."

"Assistant Commissioner," Marsden shouted into the handset. "Where are you?"

"HQ," said Collins. "I'm all right."

"Thank God," said Marsden quite sincerely. Collins was touched.

"Thanks," he mumbled, feeling something of an embarrassment. "Are you able to access files?"

"Yes," said Marsden. "I am at the office - we were all recalled."

"The glued boot print," said Collins. "What size was it?"

He heard Marsden strike the keys for a few minutes.

"Forty-two, metric," answered Marsden. "Anything else, sir?"

"Not for now," Collins told him. "Stay within range."

"Yes, sir," said Marsden. "Stay safe, will you?"

Collins replaced the phone in his pocket.

"I need to check something," he told the gathering.

He rode the lift back to his office and sat down at his desk, placing the unshaven chin onto large hands.

There was no apparent connection, he told himself. None – and yet he knew there was one. A raid on a shack owned by ASIO. A murder at a picket line and a provocation at a protest march. Without knowing who lived in that shack, I cannot connect these three dots. Now a fourth – a disease outbreak at a Russian Embassy. A fourth dot or completely unrelated?

He lifted the phone on his desk and frowned, hearing the chirp of the voice mail system. His standing orders were for all messages to be conveyed to him immediately.

He dialled his pin combination.

"One new voice mail mesage. Press one to play new messages."

He thumbed the key on the pad.

"Assistant Commissioner, this is Deakin. We spoke earlier this evening. I want you to call me at home."

Collins wrote down the meticulously enunciated number and erased the message.

He used the cell phone to call Deakin's home.

"Deakin," said a slightly breathless young voice.

"What's going on?" asked Collins without a preamble.

"Things aren't so good," Deakin's voice cracked with panic. "My wife is a nurse in intensive care. She is in isolation - they say she was exposed to something very dangerous."

"I am sorry," said Collins simply. "I hope it will blow over."

"Thank you," Deakin regained control, his voice now stronger and calmer. "Look, I wasn't happy about what happened."

Collins waited in silence.

"I don't mean to be disloyal, but I could see that something wasn't right," Deakin continued. "I called the archive where we store paper files to check - and got lucky."

"Go on," said Collins neutrally.

"The property was cross-referenced in another file, listing the surviving defectors from Communist countries," explained Deakin. "It said there is a paper file relating to the matter. I took down the number and went to look for it."

"What did it say?" asked Collins genially.

"Three weeks ago it was requisitioned in a batch of other files," said Deakin. "By the Office of Prime Minister and Cabinet."

"Three weeks ago," mused Collins. "They should have been returned immediately."

"That's the thing," said Deakin. "There was an incident in the building where they were temporarily housed. Some kind of electric fault, and the safe caught fire."

"What kind of crap is this?" marvelled Collins. "A safe catching fire?"

"Well, it wasn't a proper safe, apparently. Some kind of an alarmed steel cabinet with lots of space and lots of air. Once the wiring fault ignited the contents, the water from the sprinklers failed to get inside. All the documents were burnt beyond restoration."

"Do you believe any of this?" asked Collins incredulously.

"Not a word, Assistant Commissioner. I wasn't sure what to make of this, then I heard from my wife. She is in isolation, but she was able to use her cell phone."

"What did she say?"

"One thing of value. The man who died in the hospital - the index case, they call him. He was Russian, and he came from the embassy."

"I know that," Collins told him. "So what did you make of that?"

"Well," Deakin hesitated. "The raided shack housed an Eastern Bloc defector. We don't have many left alive, and they are all from USSR."

"All right," said Collins. "A raid on a Russian defector three days ago. A sick man in the Russian embassy. What's the connection?"

"That I can't tell you," said Deakin honestly. "But don't you think? Two highly unusual events close together? Coincidence?"

"See your point," Collins told him. "I don't believe in coincidences. Do you?"

"No way," said Deakin firmly.

"You did right to tell me," said Collins. "If there's any trouble, let me know. You are on solid ground legally - state of emergency and all that. Stay inside and keep safe. Well done."

"My wife was exposed to that shit," Deakin told him. "I am past tribal loyalties."

###

Arnold caught up with him in the car park, grabbing Collins by the arm. There was still plenty of strength in the old man, thought Collins, as his body was spun around with some force.

"Explain yourself."

"I am checking a lead."

"Without telling me? Jim, this is not a circus. A national emergency is in progress, and my most senior subordinate is prancing out into the night like some cowboy in a theme park. What are you doing?"

"I can't tell you."

Arnold's features creased in frustration.

"I don't want to pull rank you, Jim."

"Then don't."

"Please, Jim. You can't act like a teenager at a time like this. What the fuck is wrong with you?"

Collins held up his hands in conciliation.

"Flynn, let me tell you what I can. I received a lead. It's not a strong lead, but it has to be chased to the ground because it's the only one we have."

"So far so good."

"I can't tell you the rest."

"Why the fuck not?"

"I can't tell you that either. But if you stop me, there may be hell to pay. If it turns out to be right connection, we only have a short time to nail it."

"You will need to account for it in full."

"Let me check it out, then I am all yours. It will take less than an hour."

Arnold let his arms drop to the side and stared at Collins for a few seconds. Then he motioned Collins to the car park, turned on his heel and shambled back inside the building. Collins watched the glass doors slide apart, then got into the car.

There was an armoured personnel carrier outside the main entrance to Parliament. Collins was stopped by a patrol of armed troops and asked to step out. He was searched and driven the remainder of the distance in an open-topped Land Rover.

Security was paranoid, with soldiers in full battle kit every few yards. Holding up his badge for all to see, Collins was taken up in the lift and escorted down the corridor by two soldiers with assault rifles at the ready. Their boots made deep impressions in the plush carpet. Collins recalled the glued boot print, and his mouth tightened with anger.

Reilly met him at his desk, looking less than his elegant public persona. He wore jeans and a light striped shirt, crumpled and redolent of sweat. He did not appear to have shaved for some hours.

Stahl was at his side, still dressed in his customary suit. The sole concession to the emergency was absence of tie, the tail of which protruded from the breast pocket.

"Assistant Commissioner," said Reilly genially. "I don't recall meeting you before."

"We hadn't met, Prime Minister," confirmed Collins with a neutral expression.

Reilly shifted slightly, as if he changed his mind about shaking hands.

"How can we be of help?"

"I will come to the point," said Collins. "A few weeks ago your office requisitioned a number of old files from ASIO."

"If you say so - we are kind of busy right now," replied Reilly, frowning.

Collins couldn't fail to see the lines appearing in the round face, and he felt the hunter's quickening pulse.

"One of them describes a matter of interest to a recent investigation," he uttered, peering into Reilly's face intently. "I am told the said file was lost in some kind of office fire."

Reilly snapped his fingers in frustration. "That was a ridiculous incident. A short-circuit in the alarm system - can you believe it?"

Collins studied the round face as he chose his reply.

"With difficulty."

His answer hung heavily in the air. Reilly raised his hands in supplication.

"It seems that nothing is safe from progress."

"So it seems," said Collins. "I therefore wonder, Prime Minister. I wonder."

"What about?" asked Stahl irritably. "Can you get to the point?"

"I wonder whether you had time to peruse those files," said Collins. "I am desperate to learn who lived in Blackie's Creek."

"Where?"

"It's a spot in Gippsland, Prime Minister. One little shack in a desolate valley – owned, strangely enough, by the Attorney-General's Department. As in, ASIO. Three days ago it was attacked by persons unknown."

"So what happened?" asked Stahl keenly.

Collins turned to him and bored into the dark eyes.

"The occupant appears to have escaped," he replied. "Does that tell you something, Mr Stahl?"

"Nothing whatsoever," replied Stahl defiantly. "I just wondered if I heard something like that on the news. The Prime Minister's Office didn't get a chance to study those files before the fire. It's all in the office log."

"What a pity," said Collins gravely. "Is there anything else you can tell me?"

"Like what, sir?" asked Reilly in exasperation. "Please don't play riddles."

"Like whether anyone else was able to copy those files and pass them to an outside source," said Collins slowly and coldly.

Reilly moved away from his desk, rising to his full height.

"How dare you," he said breathlessly.

"I am just a simple policeman," Collins told

him. "And these are facts."

"The computerized version of the file is conveniently corrupted, and the paper version disappears in some kind of Mickey Mouse office fire. Check."

He looked from one man to the other and continued.

"The shack that is referenced in the file is understood to house a Russian defector. I know that from other sources. Check."

Stahl rolled his eyes in a gesture of impatience, which Collins utterly ignored.

"Then we have the picket line murder and a bloodbath at a union march," he continued mildly. "Actually, that's what I was working on."

He could see that both now studied him with rapt attention. Instinct, he thought, instinct. Truly, there is no better tool.

"We have reasons to believe that the raid on the shack was carried out by the people who committed the strike murders. In that light, a requisition of the relevant document by your office becomes highly significant."

Stahl smiled coldly and stepped up to Collins.

"Tell me, Assistant Commissioner," he said

slowly, in a hoarse, loud whisper. "Are you, by chance, afraid?"

"Very," replied Collins coldly. "But not of vermin like you."

"That is a great mistake on your part," said Reilly.

Collins turned, studied Reilly for a moment and nodded. He turned abruptly on his heels and ran towards the doors.

"What the fuck?" shouted Reilly.

Collins flung open the door.

"Guards!" he screamed at the top of his voice.

Even the plush carpet could not stifle the hammering of boots as three soldiers burst into the office, rifles at the ready.

"Radio the senior officer," bellowed Collins, holding up his badge.

"He has no right to give you orders!" shouted Stahl.

The soldiers stared in confusion for a few seconds, then one of them reached for the radio pouch.

"Stop!" shouted Stahl, surging forward.

The other two stepped between Stahl and the soldier with the radio.

"With respect, sir," said the soldier with the radio. "No one here has the right to give us direct orders. We respond as we see fit."

No one spoke until a lean, dark-haired officer burst into the room, radio in hand and breathless from the run.

"Identify yourself," said Collins, holding up his badge.

"Captain Saunders, Third RAR. I am in charge of this sector."

"Very good, Captain. Check my badge and listen carefully. I had come here to ask Mr Reilly and his offsider a number of questions pertaining to a murder investigation. In the course of the discussion they began to threaten me."

Saunders stared in momentary confusion, then nodded his understanding.

"What do you want me to do, Assistant Commissioner?"

"I want you to enter what I told you in the log."

"But I wasn't here for that conversation."

"No, you weren't. I just want you to enter what I said now. In case something happens to me before I finish that investigation. Get it?"

Saunders' young features tightened with anger as he shifted his gaze from Collins to Reilly.

"Bet you didn't vote for him," thought Collins wryly. "Ah well, grist to the mill."

"Yes sir," replied Saunders loudly, leaving no doubt about his thoughts. "I do get it. What's next?"

"I would like an escort back to my vehicle," said Collins mildly.

Saunders stepped aside, throwing off a crisp salute. Collins returned it and walked out of the room without turning around.

Klimov sat in a small grove of pines that separated two merging freeways. The BMW was fully concealed in the undergrowth - thankfully it was a moonless night.

From that position he could observe the military patrols circling the American embassy. He was making notes with a Biro on the back of his hand. It was hoped that the pattern will emerge within the hour - he had to make the back gate without encountering any of the local authorities.

The shrill sound made him start, then frown with distaste. Klimov extracted his prepaid phone from the pocket and stared at the display, nodding sadly.

He raised it to his ear and thumbed the call button.

"Falcon, this is sparrow," said a high, distressed voice. Klimov found it in him to smile - he chose Stahl's call sign with humiliation in mind.

"Falcon," he said neutrally, still staring at the hill crowned by the statuesque profile of the American embassy.

"We have a problem," said Stahl. "Assistant Commissioner of the Federal Police barged in here asking questions about Purple Creek."

"What did he learn?" asked Klimov with academic detachment.

"Only that all records are missing."

"Which is all he can learn in the immediate term," said Klimov. "If I were you, I would be more concerned about the outbreak."

"What do I do now?" asked Stahl, sounding a little calmer.

"Your job," said Klimov with distaste. "Plus I'd discard that phone if I were you. I am about to discard mine."

"Wait a minute," rasped Stahl angrily. "You can't cut and run now. We need your help to deal with the loose ends!"

Klimov weighed his response carefully.

"There is a time to sow," he said slowly. "And a time to reap."

He turned over the phone and removed the battery, throwing both over the shoulder into the back seat. Another patrol circled the embassy; Klimov glanced at his watch and wrote down the time.

Collins raced through deserted streets. The traffic consisted of occasional police and military vehicles - he was glad he chanced to take a marked patrol car. The trip took half the usual time, and he took delight in leaving the car in Commissioner's marked space next to the lobby, keys still in the ignition.

The lift doors opened as he was crossing the lobby. Arnold left the lift and motioned Collins to stop. He marched up to him and turned him around with a forceful gesture. They walked out into the car park without speaking.

Arnold leaned against the bonnet of the car and extracted a cigarette from the pack in his hand. He held out the pack to Collins, who hesitated and took one.

Arnold produced a lighter and inhaled deeply. Collins lit his from the same flame and sucked experimentally. It's been some time since he was tempted by tobacco, and the taste was appalling. But the nicotine calm was a welcome respite from the proceedings.

"Got a call from Chief of Army," said Flynn without a preamble. "He told me what happened in Reilly's office."

Collins nodded placidly, inhaling the acrid smoke a little deeper.

"I suppose it's all true," said Flynn in a resigned tone.

"Most probably," said Collins with a voice that went hoarse from his cigarette. "Looks pretty bad as things stand."

"Fuck, Jim," said Arnold without anger. "I warned you to be careful."

"No, Flynn," Collins told him quietly and stolidly. "I will not be careful. This is still a democracy, and we still have laws. I don't care who breaks them. Whoever they are, they should expect no mercy from me."

He inhaled with a frown and blew out the smoke with force.

"What about the other way around?" asked Arnold. "What if you aren't safe from them?"

"That doesn't change what has to be done," replied Collins, crushing the cigarette under his heel. He smelled his fingers experimentally and frowned in self-disgust. "Flynn, if I go back to smoking, I will sue, and that's a promise."

Arnold smiled, gesturing with his cigarette. "Sorry, won't do it again. Don't sue - I can't afford the publicity."

Arnold threw his cigarette on the ground, stomping on it with emphasis.

"I am with you, Jim," he told Collins, proffering his hand.

Collins shook it.

"You are right," said Arnold grimly. "True enough, we play games and run intrigues. But if your suspicions turn out to be correct - as I think they will be - this goes far beyond the pale."

"Damn right," said Collins. "Now, what if this is connected to the outbreak?"

Arnold shook his head in wonder.

"Beyond belief," he replied tiredly. "But if it is, they will have to look over their shoulders for the rest of their lives. Let's hope you are wrong about that part, for their sake."

Vince Mancini crumpled the empty cup and threw it across the cipher room into the bin. He never missed, having been a semi-professional basketball player in his youth. That was how he ended up in a medium-quality college, where he walked past a naval recruitment booth. Six months later he was fitting crisp whites of the US Navy to his long frame.

The rest was history. He was now at his most important station to-date, a military attache to the embassy in Australia - a prominent outpost of American power and a probable high water mark of his service. The rest of his career would consist of staying out of the limelight and keeping a clean nose.

Which looked tricky right now. Canberra was in the grip of an emergency that smelled like novelty terrorism, according to the briefing from Langley. According to early indications, the cause was a modified virus. Annoyingly, no one in their right mind would volunteer further conclusions without further information. People on the ground just had to wait.

Australians had requested all possible help,

including the US stockpile of Zanamovir, a rarely used antiviral agent. The word was that a number of pharmaceutical companies were directed to commence large-scale production of that drug, and existing stocks will be in the air as soon as new batches come off the conveyor. One flight already landed in the local airport, left the crate on the runway and took off without so much as refuelling. Mancini was a very busy man, all these proceedings being within his brief. He was more than a little wary of the situation - adverse outcomes lurked under every bush, and that did not accord with his intended career trajectory in the slightest.

He was studying the latest traffic to emerge from decryption when the door opened after a brief knock. He looked up to see Leroy Chalmers - two hundred pounds of buffed flesh crammed into chocolate-coloured skin and clad, out of good taste, into the uniform of a Marine master sergeant.

"What is it, gunny?" asked Mancini, his voice laced with weariness. He was tired, to be sure, but the weariness mainly stemmed from Chalmers' puckered expression.

"Sir, we have a strange man at the rear gate," drawled Chalmers in his deep, melodious voice. "Says he's from the Russian embassy and he wants to speak to the military attache in private."

"Well, that's kinda hard," replied Mancini,

rubbing his sore neck. "The embassy is in quarantine."

"I told him that," said Chalmers. "So he wrote you a note."

The master sergeant stepped forward and handed Mancini a small piece of paper that was, in a better life, a car park receipt. Mancini turned it over and studied the writing on its blank face.

"The virus is a Soviet bioweapon. Will only speak inside US Embassy."

Mancini studied the note again - written in a clear hurry, but in a neat, even longhand that made aesthetic use of the available space.

Mancini nodded, ordering himself not to analyze without information. He restored the jacket of his dress uniform, straightened his tie and fitted a cap to his close-cropped skull. He followed Chalmers into the corridor, sealing the cipher room behind them.

They exited the building and walked a long way towards the rear gate. Looking over the neatly groomed garden spread over a gentle hill, they could see emergency vehicles on the freeway, their beacons slashing the darkness with red and blue flashes.

Chalmers nodded to the guards, and they held open the gate. When they reached it,

Chalmers handed Mancini a military gas mask. After a moment's fumbling, Mancini fitted it over his lean face and walked out into the street.

The man who emerged from a BMW sedan was instantly recognizable to Mancini. Cultural attache, my ass - was his reaction not three weeks ago when he read the brief. He strained his memory and recalled the name.

"Comrade Klimov, I believe," Mancini approached the BMW and stopped a few steps short, snapping a salute. "Forgive me for not coming closer - we are under quarantine."

"Understood," replied Klimov in a tone that struck Mancini with its weary gravity. "All I ask is that we move inside the gate. If I get arrested by Australian authorities, it won't be possible to use what I know."

Mancini ordered the guards to take up stations along the fence, out of hearing range. He then beckoned Klimov inside and shut the wrought iron gate with a proprietorial gesture. They were now on American soil.

Klimov spoke for a few minutes. Shortly afterwards, Mancini ran a short distance up the hill, where Chalmers stood amid the lawn like a bronze statue. His massive right hand was resting on the butt of his holstered pistol, making the 0.45 Colt look small.

"Gunny, we need to keep him safe," said Mancini, tearing the mask off his face. "Put him under guard into the garden outbuilding. Set up a secure video link inside before he goes in. Do not approach him just in case he is infectious, and I want an armed perimeter around him. I told him he will be shot if he attempts to approach any of the embassy personnel."

Chalmers nodded in comprehension.

"I don't think he means trouble, but you never know," added Mancini. "Hear me good, gunny - he is very important. Make sure nothing happens to him - yet."

Klimov's calmly stared at the flickering screen of the secure channel. There were dark circles under his eyes, and his gaze was distractedly aimed somewhere above the camera. His arms were folded in his lap, out of view.

The image was being beamed, after strong encryption, to a number of destinations throughout the world. That virtual conference-cum-interrogation saw many important people in various countries leave their beds, some not even bothering to change out of their expensive night clothes.

"Please state you name, rank and service,"

rumbled a deep voice. Invisible on the screen, a senior CIA official did not sound as if he was recently awakened.

"Lieutenant-Colonel Valeriy Klimov, formerly of the Second Directorate, FSB," replied Klimov calmly. "Presently requesting political asylum in a destination of my choice."

A faint murmur ran through the video channel.

"Gentlemen, I decided to brief you on my last operation in full. Given the facts, I believe you will agree with my desire to see the perpetrator of this hideous situation dealt with as quickly and as quietly as possible."

"I am sure you are all aware of our political situation. You understand that Russia's so-called democracy is skin-deep, and effective control still rests with power structures inherited from the Soviet era - the governing party, the military and the FSB."

"Please proceed," said the deep voice.

"You will be equally aware that the status quo lends itself to a contest for power between these three parties. The FSB held sway for the past ten years. But the drop in the oil revenues has hit very hard, and the balance is now shifting towards the military. A special forces general by the name of Vladimir Pertzov is positioning himself for a victory at the next ballot, mobilizing various reactionary elements to his cause. His army of Cossack irregulars plus a single armoured Guards division is presently engaged in operations against Islamist insurgents in the Caucasus. Pertzov's trademark is a vicious ground campaign, calculated to depopulate the Chechen region with a judicious mixture of war crimes against civilians and destruction of legitimate military targets. Pertzov's successes are winning him considerable popular appeal."

"Yes, the Russian Hitler," said a harsh female tone. Most knowledgeable observers recognized the National Security Advisor.

"That is a little grand," replied Klimov. "A cross between Pinochet and Gobbles is a more precise description. I am at liberty to say that I have little time for Petzov and so do my superiors. Most sensible observers shudder at the thought of anywhere near the world's largest thermonuclear arsenal."

"Please continue."

"The obvious aim of the current campaign is to elevate Pertzov's profile to national hero, with an eye on the forthcoming elections. It is no secret that he is angling to become a military version of the current president - a hard man supplied by Providence to take care of Russia in hard times. He will kill a quarter of a million Chechens to prove that, without breaking stride. That's just for starters."

"Why can't they get rid of him like they did with General Lebed?" asked the deep voice.

"General Pertzov has proved himself a better planner," replied Klimov. "Getting to him would require a massed assault on his headquarters, with air support and a trainload of body bags. We are essentially talking about a clash of large armies - a civil war. We cannot have that. No responsible Russian leader will do anything to provoke this scenario."

"He has a lot of support in the army, doesn't he?" asked someone.

"Oh not only within the army. Pertzov is using a tried and true recipe in our political culture. He is styling himself as a throwback to Peter the Great or Stalin, with a hungry army to back up his posturing. He espouses the concept of Greater Russia - roughly the extent of the old Czarist empire. He despises the national aspirations of former Soviet republics and openly talks about restoration of Russian rule, preferably by force. Many Russians will cheer that line of thinking. He also has a large following in former Soviet republics, where Russian minorities have been stranded under hostile regimes."

"Dreadful," said the female voice. "A seventeenth century imperialist with a thermonuclear arsenal. I can see why your superiors are frightened."

"Precisely - many Russians despise the minorities. There is a strong feeling that civilizing them was a lot of trouble, and they had no right to leave the empire. In modern times there is minimal need for physical force – most former republics can be returned to Russian rule with a mere threat of action."

"All the same, they can't wait to see the last of Russia and its so-called civilization."

"Be that as it may," answered Klimov curtly, his mouth tightening in contempt. "But we know what these flea-ridden nations did with their so-called independence. They discovered that there's more to running a country than waving placards with grammatical errors. This is not the stuff that modern success is made of."

"And your nation is?" asked the female voice quizzically.

"Just wait," said Klimov, his eyes now boring into the camera. "Give Russia twenty years under a sound leader, and it will flatten all opposition. You think that Germans and Japanese beat you in an economic war? Just wait until Russia becomes the biggest food producer on earth. Wait until its industry begins to grow at five times the rate of America's."

"Nonsense" said someone angrily.

"It wasn't nonsense in the 1860's, Vice

President," replied Klimov. "You people should thank Karl Marx for saving you from the real Russian menace - not the Armageddon delivered with rockets and tanks, but millions of private farms and thousands of factories producing cutting-edge products at minimal cost. Not German quality, perhaps, but at one tenth of the price. One day that will come to pass, and you should pray that someone like Pertzov won't be at the helm."

The reference jerked everyone back to reality. Klimov continued.

"Six weeks ago a letter reached Pertzov's headquarters. Its contents found their way to the FSB, and we were able to trace it back to an obscure individual hidden in Australia. We know him to be a mid-level defector from three decades ago. His name is Morozov - I suppose you know all that by now. What you may not know is that he was once a leading researcher in a very secret facility. In fact, I am willing to bet that he concealed his true rank."

There was a long pause on the channel, and it confirmed Klimov's supposition.

"Morozov was a virologist. He worked on Ostrov Vozrozhdenia in the Aral Sea."

"Ostrov Vozrozhdenia?" asked the deep voice. "Please confirm - is that Rebirth Island?"

"The very same," replied Klimov evenly.

"What did they do there?" asked the female voice.

"Amongst other horrors, Morozov worked on a new micro-organism in preparation for the Afghan campaign. The idea was to disseminate a totally new disease that would depopulate the Hindu Kush region. Afghanistan was required as a transit zone for invasion of Iran, and large-scale operations to maintain control of that territory were clearly considered an undesirable overhead. Morozov's group was tasked to develop an agent that would wipe out isolated communities and deprive insurgent units of food and personnel."

"Did they make progress?" asked the deep voice.

"Yes," answered Klimov steadily. "In fact, I am advised that the task was completed. They developed a new strain of the smallpox virus."

"Please expand."

"I am told that their work was extremely sophisticated, even by today's standards. The new strain produced barely recognizable symptoms before it killed, and it was effective against most individuals who were immunized with the smallpox vaccine."

"Was it tested in the field?" asked the female voice.

"Indeed. The strain was deployed at a number of remote locations in Hindu Kush. I am told that the results were devastating, the virus achieving something like nine-tenths mortality. That makes it the most lethal agent ever used in biological warfare since Tartars exported the Black Death to Europe from Crimea."

"What is required to make use of this monstrosity?"

"An infected individual must be released into the target area. Provided he or she contacts about thirty people within a week - these are figures based on the social dynamics of a middle-sized rural town - you expect to see the stated mortality rate in the region."

"What are the symptoms?"

"An overwhelming illness after an incubation period of a few days. Survivors remain extremely ill and contagious for about six weeks."

"You said that it infects those vaccinated for smallpox. Is the existing vaccine completely useless?"

"No, not entirely," replied Klimov with an ironic smile. "There is a considerable deal of protection, especially if the vaccine is administered recently. I am not an expert, but this point was specifically covered in my briefing. Most Afghans have not been vaccinated against smallpox at all. In the former Soviet Union vaccination was ceased in the late 1970's. I hope that I am immune, having been vaccinated in my childhood. But as with Afghans, the vast majority of the Chechen population has not been vaccinated, on the account of their average age - most were born after vaccination was ceased. In short, this virus is of great interest to Pertzov, whose conventional campaign has caused a lot of military casualties. It is the only thing that threatens his popularity."

"How easy is it for Morozov to get to Pertzov?"

"At the moment, very easy. The borders are hardly manned across the Black Sea region. Even if they were adequately patrolled, I doubt whether we could stop him, with Pertzov's troops running rampant all over the mountains. If Morozov makes it out of Australia, consider him home and free to do whatever he wants."

"Very well", said a measured male baritone that Klimov recognized as belonging to the president of United States. "My first question is why you are not concerned by the prospect of being charged with crimes against humanity."

"I am sure the idea has certain local ideological attraction," said Klimov calmly, as if analysing a chess problem. "However, my team has committed no such crimes. We came to Australia illegally, to be sure, but our purpose was to kill Morozov and to prevent the whole thing from happening. We had no idea that Australian authorities, not to mention their American friends, were so negligent as to allow him to retain virus stocks after defection."

There was a long silence on the channel.

"We simply couldn't imagine such laxity, and that was a mistake," explained Klimov. "It is so contrary to our mentality, which is why we did not expect Morozov to be so dangerous. We expected an ageing man armed with nothing more than a hunting rifle. But crucially, sir, it is not in your interest to allow Pertzov to reach the Kremlin. Your nation will spend the next three decades mopping up the damage to its interests world-wide."

"And what is your motivation?"

Klimov leaned forward and stared into the camera with his first display of emotion. A bitter tear ran from his right eye and trickled down the unshaven cheek. He made no attempt to wipe it, and it made a strange contrast with his voice that now became a vicious, rasping whisper.

"As you possibly know, I came to Canberra with my beloved wife of twenty-six years. She died twelve hours ago, of causes related to the outbreak."

There was a long silence.

"Second question." The President continued without any reaction to Klimov's statement. "Why is the FSB so intent on destroying the next great ruler of Russia. Why not use him?"

Klimov shook his head like a teacher stopped amid lecture by a slow pupil.

"He is not a man you control or use, Mr President. That was the great German mistake. You hunt such a man and kill him like a rabid dog before he threatens the well-being of the nation. There can be no compromise."

"Are you afraid of him?"

"Yes. I am not a squeamish man, Mr President. I served in Afghanistan and I did things that would make you nauseous. But this is different. We are not talking about psychopaths in charge of a few guns or a few planes. We are talking about the destiny of millions. Yes, I am afraid. Consider his willingness to use the virus, despite the obvious danger to population centres in Russia herself. I fear for the entire world until this man is dead."

"The next question is this," drawled the deep voice. "Why didn't you go to Australian authorities?"

"Because my people own most of them," replied Klimov with a trace of a smile on his gaunt face.

There was a murmur of indignant voices on the line.

"That's right, dear gentlemen," continued Klimov. "How could I go to Australian authorities after engineering the very disturbance that put the serving Prime Minister into office?"

There were more muffled voices and clicks, as various parties made use of video conference facilities to contact each other privately. Klimov waited, nodding his head with an ironic smile.

"And which local authorities would you have me approach?" he asked acidly. "The man in charge of Australia's spies - are you listening, Mr Stockley? You are, at best, a bumbling weasel. Imagine something like that in USA - a newly elected president comes to the CIA and asks for classified files without any explanation or accountability. Why, he would be lucky to escape an arrest, let alone impeachment. But you just hand them over and walk away clutching a ridiculous excuse."

"My former colleagues would have you cleaning toilets for the rest of your life, provided you managed to convince them that you were a fool, rather than a traitor - and that would take some doing. More likely, you would suffer a stroke during interrogation. A nine-millimetre stroke, I would opine. My former colleagues were inordinately fond of that calibre."

He paused, but there was no further challenge.

"The present Attorney-General, his immediate boss," continued Klimov pensively. "Now, he was bought for money. Gambling, as I recall. My predecessor in Canberra left a thick file of requisition documents, and that name kept cropping up. I could even name the FSB agent who had to travel to Brisbane with attache cases crammed with cash. In my country we shoot people for far, far lesser acts of treason. Frankly, I felt that the man is a useless specimen and hardly worth a cent - but the good citizens of this land thought otherwise. Amazing thing, democracy."

Unchallenged, Klimov paused. He wiped his forehead and studied the moisture on the back of his hand. He then reached past the camera, brought a glass of water to his lips and drank it in one greedy gulp.

"Forgive me," he said calmly. "I wonder if this is a start of the fever. We must continue - I have so much more of your traitors to expose. Both here and further afield - if you cooperate with me. Morozov must die, do you hear me, Mr President?"

"But he is not the only one in possession of the virus," a booming, gravelly voice came back online, and quiet murmurs went silent. "Surely his original agency still has the recipe, if not the physical stocks."

"That is almost certain," replied Klimov with a slight sigh. "But the men in charge are stolid grandparents and career officers. Neither they nor their successors would ever allow such reckless use of this weapon. Caucasus is not Afghanistan, God help us. An infected Chechen could be in Moscow or Vladivostok before he even felt unwell."

"Let us say that Morozov has triggered an unthinkable event in a country dear to us. We will cooperate with you, Colonel, and I hope you live to see the results."

"I happen to be an eternal optimist," replied Klimov drily. "But I need to speak to one man in the local law enforcement community who proved himself sound and honest. He must be brought here, and he must be allowed to speak to me in private. I would like that to happen very soon. If I am infected, there is not much time."

Collins awoke at dawn and stretched the stiff legs, throwing off the rug. He went to sleep fully clothed on top of the made bed, barely managing to throw off his shoes and cover himself with a rug from the sofa.

Penny was stretched next to him on the bed, contrary to all regulations. She yawned, baring her large fangs and flopped her chin onto his chest, staring at him with all-knowing Labrador eyes.

"You old crim," said Collins affectionately, pulling at her ear. "Why are you doing on my turf, eh?"

He looked over onto the old sofa in the corner of his bedroom.

"Oh, I pinched your rug. Fair enough. Extenuating circumstances."

He willed himself to rise and padded to the lounge, Penny following with her slightly arthritic gait. Collins poured some clean water from the kettle as she rose up at the back door and pawed the door handle he fitted with a special lever. She opened the door and pushed her tubby body past the dog-haired glass panel to the back yard.

Collins showered and put on his uniform for the first time in many months. He shaved more carefully than usual and clipped his nails, as per warning from Arnold.

At eight o'clock he was outside his cream brick unit with a small plastic bag. He used old garden shears to snip five red roses from a verdant bush in the corner of his garden. The bush survived the transplantation from the old family home he sold when Sandie died. Collins watered it religiously, in defiance of regulations. A large plastic water container was buried next to the bush in the hard dry clay. The tiny holes in the bottom dripped moisture for a few weeks at a time, ensuring that his prolonged absence from home did not threaten the survival of the plant.

He added five flaming bottlebrushes from a native bush near the porch and collected a small bag of bird seed from the veranda. He then checked the front door for the final time and walked out onto the street. Penny stared at him through the fence from the back yard, but she knew better than protest. He turned away with guilt.

The car pulled up precisely on time - his reputation for wrath was well-known amongst his subordinates. Collins climbed into the back seat, greeting the driver. He stated the first destination.

The officer with crew-cut blonde hair stared at him with some surprise. He had pale blue eyes and faded blonde eyebrows.

"It won't take long," reassured Collins.

The officer nodded and took off towards the cemetery with slightly excessive speed. It was truly not far - the new freeway vandalized one of the last bush reserves inside the city, but it reduced the journey to less than ten minutes.

Collins gave directions and winced as they bounced over the speed humps. He stopped the car next to the old maple that already began to blush with the flames of autumn, and Collins disembarked.

He walked the now-familiar path with slow certainty, a heavy weight of sorrow swelling inside his chest. He approached the tall headstone of white marble and tears sprang to his eyes as he saw the blown leaves that covered its glistening surface.

Nothing humiliates human grief like indifference of nature, Collins noted bitterly. We are born and we die - yet the sun keeps rising and setting, and uncaring clouds drift across the perfect blue of the Canberra sky. Harsh mountain winds blow dead leaves over what is left of the ones we had loved, and that is very much that.

He began to brush away the leaves with his hand. There were a couple of faded candy wrappers - he put those in his pocket.

"Excuse me, sir."

He looked over the shoulder – the driver approached respectfully, proffering a rag and a plastic water bottle. Collins took them and nodded gratefully. The driver retreated without another word.

Collins squirted water on the marble and wiped off the thick summer dust. He squirted again to make the gold lettering glitter in the tranquil morning sun.

He placed the flowers on the wet marble and filled a small stone bowl at the foot of the grave with bird seed.

"Happy birthday, Sandie."

Collins stood for a few more minutes in empty silence. He was out of tears, but the weight was still heavy inside his chest. Feeling the rising sun on his bare head, he bent down to brush the top of the headstone with his lips.

"I'll back soon."

He stowed the water bottle and the rag inside the plastic bag and walked towards the car. The engine was already running as he approached.

Collins clambered inside and fastened his belt. The vehicle began to roll, bouncing over the speed humps with much more respect for his grief.

"Has it been a while, sir?"

Collins looked up and stared at the cloudless sky for a few moments.

"Three years. Cancer."

"I am sorry, sir. I suppose you were married for many years."

"Thank you. Yes, more than thirty years. When you've been together that long, you always hope to die first. I guess I drew the short straw."

"Then you were very privileged, sir. My generation doesn't do long relationships."

Collins stared at the driver sharply, now noticing other details - the ring finger resting on the thick leather of the steering wheel was bare. There were a few wrinkles around the deep-set pale eyes, and the red rims of the eyelids spoke volumes.

"Trouble?" asked Collins shrewdly.

"`Up to my ears, sir. A custody fight on my hands at the moment."

Collins shook his head in silent disapproval.

"How old are the kids?"

"Six, four and one, sir."

"Seeing them much?"

"Not for the past three weeks," the driver

swallowed hard and stared at the road with hatred and pain.

Collins took out his notebook and wrote down a phone number and a name. He passed them to the driver, who glanced at the paper and folded it neatly with the fingers of his left hand. Collins took it from the lean hand and gently placed it inside the driver's shirt pocket.

"Go see that son of a bitch," he said insistently. "He eats custody problems for breakfast. Don't wait for the problem to go away - appeasement always makes things worse. You must know that by now."

The driver took a deep breath and nodded slowly.

"Three weeks is a long time when you are little," said Collins as they approached the American compound. "Anyway, tell him I will expect results. You may be surprised how that will motivate him."

The driver stopped his powerful charge just short of the embassy gates and reached over to turn off the emergency beacon. Collins rested a heavy hand on young, powerful shoulder and briefly looked into the red-rimmed eyes. He nodded encouragement and stepped out of the car.

Mancini stood at the guard booth with a grim expression.

"Assistant Commissioner, I believe."

Collins shook hands briefly, noting that both had sweat on their palms.

"I believe your present case has been solved," said Mancini. "What a ride."

"I still can't believe it," answered Collins ruefully. "It's like a fucking dream that I can't wake up from."

"No dream, I am sorry to say," said Mancini, handing Collins a gas mask. "Everything checks out so far."

Collins shook his head with dismay and followed Mancini in silence. The walked across the expanse of the greenest lawn in Canberra and stopped short of the outbuilding. Two chairs were set on the grass some distance away, facing each other some metres apart.

"He requested total privacy, and my orders are to comply in full," said Mancini. "If you face the building and speak quietly inside your mask, the parabolics won't be able to pick it up from anywhere."

Collins nodded in agreement, the nozzle-like filters of his mask wobbling comically.

"Best of luck," said Mancini, turning on his heel.

The door of the outbuilding opened slowly. Klimov emerged into the morning light, shielding his eyes with his hand. He looked worn and aged, but not unwell otherwise.

Collins sat down on one of the chairs and removed his jacket. He loosened his tie, then thought a little and tightened it again. It was, after all, an historic occasion. Not since 1950's had a senior officer of the Russian intelligence service done anything like what Klimov was doing now.

The Russian looked like a man awakened from a deep, overdue sleep. His eyelids were red and rimmed with black circles. The broad cheeks were covered in dishevelled stubble. Yet the lips were tight with determination and pale blue eyes stared back steadily.

"Colonel," said Collins evenly.

Klimov nodded in confirmation.

"You're in a lot of trouble," said Collins.

"No thanks to you."

"Quite so," Collins chortled in grim amusement inside his mask. "I admit that we had no way of tracing you."

"I had a very professional team," said Klimov quietly and sadly. "Not professional enough, however. We came close six days ago, but Morozov proved to be unexpectedly vigilant."

"In the shack," Collins nodded affably. "Yes, I expected to find his remains there. But there is much that neither of us know about that man. Anyway, my needs are simple: I'm one overstressed policeman, and I want you, your bugs and your friends the hell out of my country. Please feel free to maim and murder each other on somebody else's soil - but we don't want you here."

The Russian looked at him and nodded bleakly.

"You know the methods of your people, and I have a lot of manpower. Let's combine our resources."

"He needs to get to the Caucasus," said Klimov. "He is probably still in Australia. Well, most likely."

Collins nodded. "If not, the game is lost."

"He has to get to the Black Sea coast," said Klimov. "An approach through either Russia, Ukraine, Turkey, Bulgaria or Romania is impossible - all those countries have been placed on high alert before my team left for Australia. Pertzov will have to get him aboard something that flies or sails from further afield."

"Flying commercially is out of the question,"

chimed Collins. "He will not be able to come near any airport anywhere in the world. I presume he can't board a private Russian flight somewhere."

"Unlikely," said Klimov. "The Caucasian Corps does not have anything long-range. Last week we had stopped all military flights out of Russia anyway. Your people need to ground all private flights out of Australia. Let's assume that he has not boarded such a flight already - otherwise it's game over."

Collins nodded, extracted a phone from his pocket and pressed a few buttons. He spoke urgently whilst Morozov went inside the outbuilding. When he returned, Collins was waiting.

"I gave the Americans photographs of Morozov," said Klimov. "Both his last available picture before defection and a photo fit. Our experts had extrapolated his ageing process and modelled what he probably looks like today. Unless your government has something more recent."

"We cannot access his file," said Collins. "Four weeks ago it was requisitioned by the Prime Minister's department, I had just been told, and they appear to have lost it in a small fire."

"Such carelessness," said Klimov, shaking his head with mock surprise. "Office fire, for heaven's sake. Just like the Reichstag."

"That's right," replied Collins savagely. "Except for the outcome."

"Hopefully," parried Klimov. "Tell me one thing before we continue."

Collins nodded grimly.

"The embassy," said Klimov.

"No survivors," said Collins flatly. "I am very sorry."

Klimov raised his eyes to the blue sky and stared at its bright desolation for a few minutes.

"Let's continue," he said harshly.

"Most likely, we are talking about sea transport," said Collins. "He may have made his escape as early as five days ago - correct?"

"Yes," answered Klimov. "But unlikely. He could not have pre-planned it in such detail. What does it take to board a ship as an illegal passenger?"

"Go to a large port and negotiate with a skipper of any vessel that looks dodgy."

"He would not risk flying to a port city," mused Klimov. "Yet time is of the essence."

"That means trying either Sydney or Melbourne. Also Wollongong, and Corio. The rest are just too far to take the risk."

"The vessels already departed in the past four days will need to be boarded at sea," nodded Klimov.

Collins redialled the number and issued further instructions.

"Could be tricky," he said gruffly. "If they are in international waters, it takes a lot of dancing. What else?"

"Let's assume that he is still here," said Klimov. "Where would he go?"

"Any of these four places. Or he may have hidden somewhere to wait this out," said Collins.

"He will be under tremendous pressure to leave. Over here he is wanted for mass murder. In Pertzov's headquarters he is a hero. He will be making every effort to get there, and Pertzov will be making every effort to assist from his end."

"Is he likely to have the virus with him?"

"He must have a small stock of it," said Klimov. "It may look totally innocuous - pen, tie pin, watch, even glasses."

"That tiny?"

"He infected my man through a very small projectile, fired from a .22 rifle," said Klimov. "In theory an object the size of a sand grain would do the job. Biological weapons are repulsive."

"You aren't one to talk," growled Collins, tapping his mask.

"Why is that?" glared Klimov defiantly. "I did not order that filth to be engineered. Don't play virgin, my dear colleague. All nations do sickening things in war - and they are none too scrupulous in peace either. The Americans have a bioweapons programme, and so do the Chinese. We simply had better scientists than anyone else."

"What else can you think of, Colonel?"

Klimov chuckled at the mention of his rank, now clearly obsolete.

"Morozov must be taken by surprise," he replied. "I would not alert the ships. I would board each one by helicopter, then sweep as fast as possible and be prepared to isolate anyone who may be shot by what appears to be a small, low-velocity projectile. The assault teams should wear gas masks to avoid aerosol-borne infection."

Collins nodded. "Anything else?"

"I will think of something, I am sure, and I will notify you as I do. Now please excuse me - I must rest to be of further use. Come back in a few hours - here's a list of what need."

###

"Nothing so far," said Klimov with finality. He threw down the printouts on the grass and sat back with a defeated look in his eyes. He thought for a few minutes and looked up. "He could be right here in Canberra, for all we know."

"I fucking hope not," replied Collins with alarm. "That would be bad."

"I am sorry," said Klimov. "But I haven't been thinking. It's time to get into the enemy's head: basic strategy."

"You start," said Collins. "After all, you understand him better. We have no real information about Morozov - it appears as if he lived with virtually no contact with authorities or anyone else. In other words, whatever you have on him from Soviet days is probably all we have to work with."

"Very well," said Klimov. "First, let's paint a thumbnail sketch of a man. Military physician, marathon runner and marksman by way of extracurricular activities."

"Has he had training in covert procedures?"

"No, and that's an important point. He was a practising military surgeon, and then he was co-opted into research. Apart from basic infantry training required of an officer, he has no skills or experience relevant to what is happening to him now."

"He defects and spends a year in America being interrogated," chimed Collins. "He sticks to his story of being an administrator of the Rebirth Island facility and gives Americans a lot of airy stuff about what goes on there - but no real details. Says he didn't have a full security clearance, claims that he administered requisitions, personnel, maintenance. After debriefing they ship him here, he spends another year in a safe house in Queensland - then his chief handler retires and buys a cheese factory in Bairnsdale. It's time to let Morozov out of the cage anyway, so they build him a shack in the bush not far from his handler, who hires him to do a little work in the factory lab. Quality control and all that. Opinion has it that he could have replenished his virus stock there. He must have had the templates."

"He is likely to have concealed them on his person," said Klimov. "A special container was manufactured for covert handling of such objects, and his laboratory was known to have them. A small incision is made in the scrotum, and the object is attached to the inside of the skin with a single stitch. Due to the nature of the scrotal skin the incision becomes invisible.

It is made of light silicone rubber that is almost invisible on X-Ray. That is how he probably concealed it all along."

"After the former controller succumbs to old age, the factory is sold and eventually goes bankrupt," continued Collins. "It appears as if its finances were never much good, and the next owner failed to improve them. Morozov is now unemployed, bored and angry."

"When did that happen?" asked Klimov.

"Six years ago."

"So he broods, maybe drinks a lot - but soon realizes that he can't drown his basic needs. His thoughts turn to Russia."

Collins nodded in agreement.

"It's a changed country, and he sees new possibilities that were totally out of the question under the Soviet rule. He begins to travel to Melbourne to buy Russian magazines and DVD's. The owners of the Russian shops begin to recognize him, and more than one has shipped orders to a post box in Bairnsdale. "

"Eight weeks ago General Pertzov receives the now famous missive and makes preparations to have Morozov repatriated."

"Four weeks later Morozov withdraws fifty thousand dollars from his bank account in cash to buy a boat – or so he tells the bank manager."

"Five days ago we raid his shack but run into a competent perimeter defence. Morozov escapes into the bush, apparently kitted out in readiness for an attack, and we lose track of him after that."

Both men fell silent and looked at each other intently.

"Let's go back to that moment," said Klimov. "He wakes up to the alarm, escapes from the house carrying a gun and a backpack with whatever he needs. He shoots one of my men and thus sets in train the epidemic - probably intending to distract the authorities from his escape."

"Yes," agreed Collins. "So what would you do next in his shoes?"

"What would I do? I am alone in the bush. I must find a way to get onto some transport immediately. I have to get clear of the area and the assault team that is after me. Within weeks after that I have to get out of the country. A wanted mass murderer here. In Pertzov's camp I am awaited as a hero. I must get there – it's that simple."

"And in that situation he is helpless," said Collins. "He knows that he can't leave legally, and he has to assume that those hunting him know more about border control than he does. Any amateurish attempt to leave is likely to end in failure."

"Much smarter to call for help," replied Klimov. "Yes. We are looking for a call to Russia within hours or maybe days of my team's attack. The call would be brief and may have been repeated from another location a day or so later. He would be told that he must move immediately after using either a landline or a cell phone. He probably doesn't have a car and uses other transport to get around."

"In this area that will have to be a bus," said Collins. He lifted his phone and issued a number of orders.

"Back to the other side of the ocean." continued Klimov. "Pertzov receives a frantic call for help. He will curse and shout, then order someone to fix the problem or else he will have their balls for breakfast. At least two men will be despatched to Australia to meet Morozov and get him out of the country."

"Which takes us back to trying to board a ship," said Collins.

"Most likely," replied Klimov. "Unless..."

"What?"

"Wild thought. He may try to use a submarine if one is handy."

"Can they be located?"

"Not by you, no. Australia has an extensive radar screen for air traffic, but no sonar network in its territorial waters. Barring an accident, submarines slip in and out entirely undetected. Once surfaced, they may be caught on a satellite image, but it is too late to act by the time this information is processed. Bottom line is, Australia does not have the resources to stop such a vessel from entering its coastal waters."

"How close to shore can they approach?"

"So close you can swim to them in a few minutes. It is better to use an inflatable craft from the submarine, They prefer to remain off the littoral so they can submerge if required. It all depends on whether a submarine is available to Pertzov and whether he could get it into local waters quickly enough. The whereabouts of submarines are, of course, a closely guarded secret. Even my former superiors would have difficulty obtaining that information. Given the rivalry between services, in fact, I would not be surprised if the matter reached the President's office before the inquiry was answered. Mind, any information is likely to be days old and therefore inaccurate. Submarines do not report their position like surface ships."

"So am I hearing you correctly? Are we

looking for a few helpers who flew into the country recently?"

"Yes, I believe so. Look for two to three men with Estonian, Latvian or Lithuanian passports on the same flight, seated away from each other, aged between thirty and forty-five. They will arrive within forty-eight hours of the phone call."

"Why from there?"

"These nations are now members of the European Union, and their citizens don't have to apply for a visa to get to Australia. There are many ethnic Russians who are poorly treated by their governments. Pertzov has many angry men from that contingent to call on."

"What is the likely route?"

"Frankfurt, Asia - then here."

Collins lifted his phone and added to the list of previous instructions.

Klimov was busy reading through the printouts. Collins looked around the room with curiosity.

"You know, I've never been inside the American embassy before," said Collins. "They sure do things in style, don't they?"

"Baubles," answered Klimov curtly "Our embassy isn't even painted properly, but we subverted your country from that dowdy compound for five decades."

He went back to the printouts whilst Collins studied the ornate ceiling fixtures.

"So why don't you paint it?" asked Collins suddenly.

Klimov looked up and smiled sadly.

"Now, that's the difference between my civilization and yours," he explained. "See, the Germans got to the eastern shores of the Baltic and what did they do? Build pretty castles and cities. We, on the other hand, just pushed in all directions out of Moscow until we owned one sixth of the world's dry land. Didn't stop to paint anything or make it pretty - and when the time came, we took the pretty Baltic cities from the Germans into the bargain. You, Westerners, settle down and work hard to make things nice. We, Russians, conquer - and when we get sick of the shabby view, we get up and conquer more."

He went back to studying the printouts as Collins pondered the pronouncement and maintained a patient silence.

Twenty long minutes later Klimov stood up and tore a sheet from the printout. Collins rushed towards him as Klimov neatly underlined two names with a felt pen.

"Speaking of pretty German cities on the Baltic," he said lightly. "Look here."

Collins bent down to study the printouts.

"This one and this one," continued Klimov. "They get on a plane in Tallinn and fly to Frankfurt. Separate seating."

Collins nodded.

"Six hours later they board a flight for Singapore, this time sitting together."

Collins reached for his phone.

"Four hours after arriving to Singapore - that's too fine for any pre-booked connections - they get on a Qantas plane, business class, probably on standby. Seats away from each other again. Disembark in Sydney."

Collins thumbed a well-used key on his phone and spoke a few words to Marsden. He spelled the long names awkwardly and looked up at Klimov.

"Now, these men would have landed cold. There is no network of any kind for them to rely on," said Klimov loud enough to be heard on the other end. "They will either buy or rent a vehicle. Probably the latter - they cannot afford to have mechanical problems. It is unlikely that they had time to prepare false identification – therefore, they probably rented a vehicle in one of these names on the day of arrival."

"Got that," said Marsden into the phone.

Collins nodded.

"Whatever these two are up to," told him Klimov, smiling wryly. "I am sure it is of interest to local authorities."

On the signal from Collins the trooper, resplendent in his bullet-proof vest and helmet, catapulted through the glass window and came to rest in a pool of glass chips on the carpet, facing the bed. With the same fluidity he leaned forward to press the muzzle of his assault rifle to the sleeping man's ear.

The Russian awoke slowly and froze, watching armed men surround his bed. His expression slowly tightened into a mask of absolute concentration as he studied their weapons and remained stock-still.

Collins ran into the little bedroom wheezing with effort. He watched as the prisoner was manhandled out of bed, patted down and handcuffed. At Collins' gesture the Russian was led into the lounge of the motel unit and sat down on the heavy sofa.

"Cuff him to the table," said Collins, gesturing at the heavy metal frame next to the sofa. He stood impassively as his order was carried out.

"Excuse us, boys," he told them without turning. The troopers lowered their weapons and withdrew from the room.

Collins positioned his chair in a way which allowed the men outside to see them both clearly, then leaned forward to study the prisoner. The Russian looked like a man awakened from a deep, long-overdue sleep. His eyelids were red and rimmed with black circles. The cheeks were covered in dishevelled blond stubble. Yet the lips were tight with determination, and pale blue eyes stared back steadily.

"Mr Kolesnikov, I believe," said Collins evenly. The prisoner stared back blankly.

"You're in a lot of trouble," said Collins.

"I want a lawyer."

"Don't worry about us," smiled Collins. "Worry about your boss. Now, he will be very unhappy, and I hear that General Pertzov is a bad man to disappoint."

"Who?" The Russian chortled as if amused and looked away.

"Please don't waste my time."

"Whoever you are," said Kolesnikov quietly and vehemently. "Please shoot me and spare me the speeches. I don't care about dying - but please get on with it."

"I am not here to kill anybody," said Collins reasonably. "Look, I'm just a very stressed policeman. I want you, your resentments and your friends the hell out of my country."

The Russian looked at him and shook his head bleakly.

"I don't understand what you are talking about. I am a tourist."

"Look, tourist. Our American friends can get it out of you with chemicals. Hell, we can get your Russian buddies to do that. But that would mean dragging you back to Canberra. I don't have time."

"I understand your dilemma," said Kolesnikov with utter disinterest, the alarm in his eyes fading. He looked out the window.

"Well, it may interest you to know that my superior has authorized me to kill you. On sight, in fact."

"Is that supposed to frighten me?" asked Kolesnikov unenthusiastically.

"Yes, it should. See, we can put you on a plane to Russia with FSB escort. It will land in Moscow, where you won't need to guess your fate for too long. If you have a family, I would start thinking," said Collins. "All of the embassy personnel had died. The FSB are very angry."

"Why didn't you send me there already?"

"I resent you being here, but I still want you to leave this country unharmed. We can make a deal: I suspect your family is in Estonia somewhere. It's not impossible to evacuate them before Pertzov discovers what happened to your mission."

Kolesnikov stared at Collins intently.

"I am offering you asylum," said Collins. "Not here - it's not safe enough. But Americans will rehouse you in a quiet neutral country. A man with your skills will land on his feet."

Kolesnikov moved to bring his hands up to his face, but the handcuffs jarred his right wrist. He shook his head in annoyance.

"What is the time?" he asked.

"Zero six fifty."

"Almost midnight in Estonia," said Kolesnikov quickly. "Here's my offer. I will phone them now, and they will be admitted inside the American embassy in Tallinn for evacuation to a neutral destination. Meanwhile, you will take me to the American embassy in Canberra, and I will give you Morozov."

"Too slow. I need him now."

"Sorry. I have no reason to trust you, and you have every reason to want me dead. It's my way or nothing."

"Is there enough time?"

"Yes, yes. Days."

Collins thought it over slowly.

"Very well," he said, signalling to the troopers in the street. "I need the key."

The trooper gave him a long, measured look and reached into his shirt pocket. Collins took the key, unlocked the cuffs from around the sofa and snapped them on his own wrist.

"Get the helicopter ready," he told the trooper. The latter nodded quickly and left.

"Over to you," said Collins to Kolesnikov, pulling him outside.

"Call the US embassy in Tallinn to warn them. Then I will call my family. By the time we get to Canberra, they should be safe. I will confirm this and then we talk."

Collins nodded, phone already in hand. He dialled Mancini and waited for the American to come on the line.

"Another favour needed from Uncle Sam," he told him apologetically. "Hope your taxpayers can afford it."

Klimov gave Kolesnikov a long stare.

"You cannot possibly be lying," he said contemptuously. "I don't think you have the brains to make this up."

"It is all true," Kolesnikov ignored the insult. "You badly underestimated Pertzov, clever boy."

Klimov shook his head and looked up at Collins ruefully.

"This is becoming complicated."

"So I see," nodded Collins. "A naval vessel under the Russian flag but really on a pirate mission - all a bit messy legally. In our territorial waters, but hardly some drug ship we can just board."

"Yes, hardly," chimed in Kolesnikov. "It can torpedo most of your navy before you even detect it. I served on such a vessel once."

"Designation?" asked Klimov with a flicker of interest.

"Diver."

"You were thrown out of the Baltic fleet when it was decommissioned," Klimov nodded in understanding. "Then you were marooned in Estonia with your family."

"That's right," replied Kolesnikov. "Treated like dogs ever since, while Mother Russia looked away and did nothing."

"Pertzov's ready fodder," confirmed Klimov. "He has thousands like you."

"Millions," answered Kolesnikov with a defiant stare. "All he needs is a little time."

Klimov put his hands on the coffee table and leaned to stare at Kolesnikov with hatred.

"Which I will deny him," he whispered harshly. "That, Comrade, I promise on my life."

"How do you make a submarine pick-up?" asked Collins as the waiter left.

Klimov stared at the exquisitely decorated dessert grimly. Three days ago he dined just across the road with Raisa. Their last night together - it seemed another lifetime.

He swallowed hard and looked away. It was another lifetime indeed.

"Anything the matter?" asked Collins, his tone changing to that of a seasoned policeman.

Klimov shook his head and took a deep breath. He held up his palm in a reassuring gesture.

"Nothing relevant to the problem at hand," he said hoarsely. He drained the rest of his wine and continued.

"First criterion: no large ports, especially naval ones, nearby."

"That's most of the south coast, from Bateman's Bay to Eden."

"Long, shallow littoral is bad," said Klimov. "Submariners like depth below them, at least thirty fathoms. That way they can approach and retreat under water."

Collins made a note on a sheet of paper.

"Deep bays are therefore ideal," continued Klimov. "The subject is usually collected by inflatable boat, so beaches with heavy surf are not convenient. The inflatable is piloted from the submarine - typically by two divers, like our friend Kolesnikov - or the subject motors out to sea in their craft. However, the latter is not the preferred method - if the craft is missed or found empty at sea, it attracts unwanted attention."

"So we are looking for a bay with a quiet beach and deep sea offshore," said Collins. "What - two, three men in diving suits on an inflatable?"

"One or two. Black suits, spear guns of the crossbow type, diving knives. Electric motor on the boat - more reliable in rough weather and almost silent."

Collins made further notes.

"The rendezvous is always at night," added Klimov. "Early hours of the morning are preferred. The sub surfaces briefly to launch inflatable, then submerges to reduce the likelihood of being seen. The inflatable stops a few hundred feet offshore and waits, totally silent and invisible in the dark. The subject signals, usually by prearranged torch flashes, then the inflatable approaches and makes the pick-up. As soon as inflatable turns around, the submarine begins to surface slowly. By the time the inflatable reaches it, the tower is just above the water, and everyone gets on board. The sub then dives slowly and quietly to a safe depth and makes its getaway."

Collins made some more notes.

"We should be getting back to the embassy," said Klimov. "Mancini said he will have the tracking data by now."

Collins nodded. It was almost impossible to find submarines in open waters, but the Americans were working miracles. Satellite technology has recently marched in great strides, thanks to the efforts of Russian submarine designers.

Out of work but not out of ideas, they found employment in the foetid rivers of South America, where cocaine lords built fleets of tiny semi-submersible craft - diesel-powered coffins moving at periscope depths, invisible to traditional satellite imaging. New methods were called for, and American wizardry in electronics quickly proved equal to the task - which was bad news for all submariners world-over.

Klimov stood up and patted his full stomach.

"One moment," he said awkwardly, gesturing towards the toilet. Collins nodded to the waitress.

"Mind this, please," said Klimov, gesturing at his wallet.

The waitress came over with the bill. Collins gave her his credit card without checking the figures, and she trotted away happily. The numbers, thought Collins, contained at least one arithmetic error in favour of the house.

He reached over and poured the dregs from the bottle into his glass, hoping to have a long sleep after dinner. The next morning promised to be a very full affair, military liaisons buzzing like angry hornets.

The waitress returned. Collins opened the leather pouch and signed the credit card voucher. She smiled with joy, handed him the credit card and left.

Collins took a curious look at Klimov's wallet, lying abandoned on the table. He slowly drank the rest of the wine and checked the messages on his phone. There was no sign of Klimov.

Collins replaced the phone in his pocket and sat still, contemplating Klimov's wallet. Suddenly, he reached across and grasped the worn bundle of black leather. He leapt to his feet with force that flung his chair into the wall and ran towards the toilet, drawing curious looks from other patrons.

The toilet door led to a small, dingy corridor smelling of recent repainting and bleach. The door of the cleaning closet was ajar, and it took Collins seconds to discover that the flimsy lock has been broken. He wrenched open the door but found nothing apart from cleaning gear.

He ran into the male toilet, which was empty. Collins wrapped his heavy knuckles on the door of the female toilet. There was no reply.

He pushed open that door and stood back. There was no one inside, the only obvious finding being a mop with a broken handle, discarded on the terracotta floor.

Collins tried the window and was startled as the frame filled with frosted glass simply fell away into the narrow passage behind the restaurant. Only then did Collins see the twisted hinges, and an explosive curse escaped his lips.

He walked outside without saying a word to the waitress. Once back in the car he sat quietly, collected his thoughts and started the engine.

###

He was allowed to park next to the hangar. The old Air Force base came back to life, he noted, with helicopters, small jets and at least one American transport colossus crowding its once-deserted runways.

Collins strode inside the building, holding up his ID to the armed sentries in blue uniform. They were probably from the maintenance staff, he thought, noting how they held their rifles. They looked a bit overweight, yet ready to do whatever was necessary.

He nodded at them gruffly. It was his honour to serve too.

The briefing room was full of senior men in various uniforms. A single man stood out in that gaggle - shorter than the rest, but very broad in the shoulders, his bald head topped by a sand-coloured beret. Collins' heart started at the emblem of his old regiment - a silver dagger on golden wings with its proud motto.

"Who Dares Wins."

The man's head swivelled like a turret of a tank, and pale grey eyes locked on Collins. A hint of smile played on the fat lips as he drew to attention. The room went silent as chiefs of the Army, the Navy and the Air Force stared at the commander of the SAS - then past him, at Collins.

The former brought up a broad, meaty hand to the beret and snapped off a salute. Others followed, as if by reflex.

Collins drew himself to attention and saluted back. He then stepped forward to shake the meaty hand which nearly managed to withstand the force of his.

"General Townsend, it's been a while,"

Townsend let go and turned to others.

"Major Collins and I go a long way back," he announced in a harsh voice that betrayed more than familiarity with the bottle. "And now we all owe him, gentlemen. We owe him big."

There was a loud murmur of approval.

"But there isn't much time," said Townsend. He led Collins over to a large map of the coastline secured to the wall with small nails. "We think these are the most likely sites."

Collins looked at three red flags attached to sharp pins. One of them was inserted at a different angle to the others.

"Here," Townsend pointed at the odd flag. "The littoral is right, and there is a small, sheltered bay - the nearest habitation is miles away. The greenies fought tooth and nail until it was finally made into a national park, bless their soiled undies."

Collins smiled with a happy recollection of his days in the Regiment.

"These two other sites should also be considered," said Townsend. "The satellite has been retasked, we have Sea Kings with anti-sub capability sweeping the likely lanes of approach, and there are frigates patrolling the shoreline in between."

Collins nodded appreciatively.

"Road blocks had been prepared at regular intervals along the coastal highway," he replied. Two unmarked cars, three officers in each. Full set of tactical response gear. We will make sure that he doesn't get to shoot."

"What if he does?" asked an Air Force general, whose name Collins was struggling to recall.

"We have the antiviral drug on standby," replied Collins. "Better chance than being shot with a conventional round, anyway."

"What are your plans for the arrest?"

Collins nodded grimly.

"The Americans will take the prisoner and any samples he may have," he replied. "I have their insistent request not to kill him. Frankly, that sticks in my throat - but a deal's a deal."

An older man of huge stature with a broad, open face approached Collins. The green uniform with general's epaulettes was beginning to get tight around the waste, but the massive arms with a few faded tattoos still bulged with muscle.

"Jim, old friend," he said, shaking Collins by the hand. Tell me whether it's all true. You know all of us here, and you know what our country means to us. We need to hear it from you."

Collins stared into the man's hazel eyes, still holding his hand steadily.

"I am sorry, General Landgrove," he replied steadily. "So far all the facts appear to tally."

Landgrove squeezed lightly and let go, shaking his head in grief.

"We have all sworn an oath," he said softly. "You must tell us if you need help to uphold yours."

Collins felt ice inside his stomach. That's why they are all here, he thought frantically. All the branches of the armed services and I, from the Federal Police. All the king's men. Has it really come to that?"

"That won't be necessary," he replied loudly and firmly.

Landgrove let out a sigh and put a heavy hand on his shoulder.

"I will go with your assessment," he said with finality. The room remained silent.

Townsend cleared his throat.

"Everything is in place," he said softly. "All we do now is wait."

"Group six, we have a contact," whispered an angry male voice on the speaker. Collins put down his paper cup, spilling a few drops of coffee. Townsend straightened next to him, crushing the cigarette in the ashtray and pressing it into the ash with his stubby finger. He held it there for a moment, then pushed the ashtray away.

"Group eight, we copy," whispered a reply. "Black inflatable, two men, approaching the shore at around three knots."

There was tense silence on the radio.

"Group eight, another contact on the beach," the whisper was now even quieter. "One male, looks unarmed."

Collins tapped Townsend on the sleeve.

"I need a description."

Townsend placed his finger over a button on the headset and cleared his throat, pressing a handkerchief over his mouth. He stared at the handkerchief briefly and angrily crumpled it in his fist.

"Command one to group six. Describe land contact."

"Group six, contact on the beach is male, late thirties, thin build. Blonde hair, short beard, black tracksuit. No backpack, hands free."

Collins swore softly.

"That's not Morozov," he said loudly. "They need to wait - he must be hanging back."

Townsend nodded.

"Command one to group six," he thumbed his headset. "The primary target is in his fifties, overweight. Don't move until he appears."

"Group six, copy," whispered the reply. Townsend turned off his headset and looked at Collins.

"But we can't just let him go," he said uncertainly.

Collins thought furiously.

"No," he replied at long last. "Take him if the inflatable begins to depart without Morozov."

Townsend nodded.

"Command one to group six, seven and eight," he said into the microphone. "Apprehend if the inflatable takes off with no further contacts appearing."

Three acknowledgements were whispered in numerical order. Collins glanced at the handkerchief protruding from Townsend's fist. Crimson spots were clearly visible on the cloth.

Collins stared at the blood, and his gaze involuntarily shifted to the ashtray in front of his old commander.

"Group six, contact is signalling with a small flashlight."

Collins turned to Townsend and gave him a long appraising look. The meaty face was still broad and brawny, but there were new angles, and the large shaven head had changed colour. Even the ancient lighting of the briefing room couldn't hide the lemon-sallow hue.

"Group six, inflatable has beached. Land contact running towards inflatable."

Townsend's sausage finger hovered on the microphone button.

"Group six, contact has boarded the inflatable. One man from inflatable is in the water."

Collins tensed up, and his mouth opened as he inhaled.

"Group six, inflatable being pushed out to sea."

Townsend triggered the microphone.

"Group six, apprehend!"

The speaker exploded with noises - shouts, running feet, heavy breathing and spits of muffled gunfire.

"Group seven, man down, man down!"

"Group six, contacts apprehended. Two dead."

"Who is dead?" shouted Collins.

Townsend leaned forward.

"Command one to group six. Identify the dead."

"Group six, one of the divers from the inflatable bought it after he fired a spear at our squad leader, thigh penetration. We have the bleeding under control. The land contact got caught in the cross fire. Both confirmed kills."

"Evacuate the beach and take the inflatable with you," said Townsend. "Command one to group five, come in."

"Group five, copy."

"Get out without lights," ordered Townsend. "I want the evac to be invisible from the sub."

"Group five, copy."

Townsend turned off the microphone and turned towards Collins.

"That's that," he said apologetically.

"Yeah," said Collins thoughtfully. "We will see what Mr Kolesnikov has to say."

Kolesnikov smiled defiantly.

"My family is quite safe," he told Collins. "And where is your traitor friend?"

Collins ignored the taunt.

"No, your family is not safe," he explained patiently. "If your attitude doesn't improve, Americans will hand them over to Russian authorities, not even Estonians."

"Feel free," said Kolesnikov. "I don't know those people. As I said, my family is quite safe - in Vladivostok. When the fleet was decommissioned, I wasn't."

"We can use chemicals," said Collins gruffly.

"Might be an interesting experience for both of us," replied Kolesnikov. "But I can't tell you what I don't know. We came here to rendezvous with Morozov and to keep him safe. Then Pavel was to go with him somewhere, and I was to leave on the submarine. When you arrested me, Pavel took my place. I have no idea what he did with Morozov, but I am sure it was creative."

Collins stared at him in horror.

"You will be tried and punished to the full severity of our laws," he told Kolesnikov.

The man smiled and beckoned Collins towards him. Collins leaned forward, knowing that the prisoner was securely handcuffed to the seat.

"I know your western jails," said Kolesnikov. "I am so looking forward to having meat for breakfast, lunch and dinner. You see, I spent twenty years on nuclear submarines, sleeping on sweaty bunks and inhaling leaking radiation. I ate food that would make you vomit and I breathed air that would make your eyes water."

He leaned back and smiled.

"My family will be told that I died and went to heaven," he added dreamily. "Mother of God, that will only be true."

The briefing was reconvened in Parliament at Reilly's insistence. Collins smiled wryly when notified of this with a terse text message. The man likes to play dangerously, he thought. By now, surely, he will be informed that all the Armed Forces chiefs know about Klimov's allegations.

Collins balled his giant hands into fists. Klimov's disappearance made a lie out of every word he uttered, even though Collins was reasonably certain that most of it was true. But without a single shred of other evidence to confirm it, Klimov's absence made an act of high treason a non-indictable offence.

As he rode the elevator to the top floor, Collins weighed up spilling the story to the media. It was an easy thing to spill, he argued, but what editor would publish such an outrage? It was the simplest thing in the world to allege that Klimov was a plant, working to divert attention in much the same manner as the stunt with the submarine diverted attention from Morozov's real departure – wherever that took place.

Collins was searched for a weapon and smiled wryly when security guards unscrewed his heavy pen.

"Be careful," he said lightly. "It writes."

That earned him a scornful look, which he utterly ignored.

There were over forty men seated around a long table - the entire cabinet, chiefs of staff and others - Arnold in his resplendent persona, clad in a crisp uniform bedecked with decorations, the head of Customs and Stockley, who stared at Collins acidly. Reilly and Stahl sat at the opposite end of the table; both pretended that they were studying papers.

Others looked at him with impatience as Collins strode towards the table, nodding his greetings. He took his time and sat down slowly, folding hands in front of him on the mahogany surface.

"So here we are, gentlemen," he drawled resonantly. "All the effort, all the expenses, all the king's men. And the result is: nothing."

"You sound almost pleased with the fact," remarked Stahl curtly.

"It's always a pleasure watching professionals at work," replied Collins with levity. "We are now down to our last options."

He opened his hands and began to flex fingers as he enumerated the options.

"There is no commercial marine traffic - the continent is quarantined. All cargo and passenger ships are at anchor in port."

"With many complaints," confirmed Reilly.

Collins nodded at him radiantly.

"It is impossible for any man matching Morozov's description to come anywhere near an airliner."

"What about private aircraft?" asked the head of Customs.

"Certainly, all had been warned," said Collins. "That doesn't exclude the possibility of an internal flight, but private flights to overseas destinations had all been grounded."

"That is correct," said a bald man in the far end of the table. Collins squinted at him questioningly.

"Apologies, I am Barry Crowley," added the bald man. "Air Traffic Control."

Collins nodded with comprehension.

"We can see all traffic, even single-engined planes," explained Crowley. "There hadn't been any attempts to leave our air space. All planes are accounted for."

"So that's air traffic," said a heavy-set man in a naval uniform. "Admiral Hawthorne, Acting Chief of Navy. There are plenty of small Australian-registered ocean-going vessels - fishing boats and yachts, for instance."

Everyone turned towards him.

"We are still watching the sub," Hawthorne continued heavily. "It departed the rendezvous point at slow speed and is presently cruising on the surface, heading 30 degrees, maintaining fifteen knots - which is slow for that kind of vessel."

"Why would it stay on the surface?"

marvelled Stahl.

"My best guess is this," said Hawthorne. "They are still trying to divert attention. They are saying - look at us, watch what we do next. Hence the slow speed. That class of vessel is capable of steaming three times faster on the surface."

"In other words, they don't intend to rendezvous with the contact?"

"Precisely. Such a rendezvous would involve a surface ship, but anything approaching the submarine would be intercepted long before it got there. They know that as well as we do, so the sub stays on the surface, showing us a false target."

"What if Morozov just holed up somewhere?" asked the head of Customs.

"Unlikely," replied Collins. "There is too much pressure to leave. He is in extreme danger of apprehension, and Pertzov is desperate to get him home safely. Every passing minute increases the likelihood of accidental detection and arrest. This man is in a deeply hostile territory, and he is valuable beyond words to Pertzov. I can't see him pitching a tent or taking out a short lease somewhere."

"That leaves us with only one likely possibility," said Hawthorne. "Departure by ocean-going vessel with Australian registration, ostensibly for a short cruise."

"Going where?" asked Reilly.

"New Zealand, Papua New Guinea, Indonesia, Fiji," recited Hawthorne quickly. "Possibly for a rendezvous with another vessel. Given the present course of the sub, I would suspect southern New Zealand - the others would take Morozov's vessel too close to the sub, whose course they know we are watching. No, we need to look in the opposite direction to the sub's - looking for any craft bearing between east and south-east, possibly even south-south-east. They may even try to circumnavigate New Zealand and rendezvous with something further in the Pacific."

"We need to liaise with the Americans," said Stockley with a fastidious expression, as if he contemplated handling raw meat. "They have better infrared capability."

"Please make these arrangements now," said Reilly courteously. The Air Force commander and Stockley stood up and began to dial numbers as they backed away from the table into far corners of the room. Others waited in silence until both returned to the table.

"We will need New Zealanders' help to apprehend, God help us," said Hawthorne. "All craft headed in their direction need to be boarded without warning, in case an attempt is made to discard the virus overboard."

"Heaven, that's unthinkable," breathed Customs. "What if it spreads to marine life?"

There was a long silence in the room. Stockley rifled through some papers in front of him.

"The people from Fort Worth didn't say anything about environmental spread," he said shakily. "But I wonder if anyone really knows what would happen."

"We can't take chances," ordered Stahl. "What is the quickest way to board such a vessel?"

"Rappel a team from a helicopter," said Townsend. "Approach just above the surface to avoid radar detection. Not that a ship of that size would have a good radar."

"The Sea King can't cross the Tasman Sea," said Hawthorne. "The best it can do is a fifth of that distance, counting a return journey. The intercept would have to come from New Zealand."

"Please excuse me," Reilly stood up and lifted the cordless phone from the table. He issued a curt order and remained standing, phone in hand. "I have to call their PM immediately."

Stockley groaned audibly, and there was a rush of murmurs in the room. Everyone remembered who was in charge in New Zealand.

"Thanks," said Reilly into his headset curtly. "Madam Prime Minister, he boomed genially. Kia Ora."

Stockley rolled his eyes, and Collins couldn't help a wry smile of sympathy.

"We have a situation here," began Reilly. He also rolled his eyes, eliciting subdued chuckles around the table. "Madam Prime Minister, that's right. And it may be coming your way."

The others listened in bored silence as Reilly admirably navigated troubled waters. Collins could only guess the other side of the conversation, and the guesses made him squirm in his seat.

There was a chirp of a mobile phone. Reilly frowned and turned away from the sound. The Air Force general scrambled to his feet and ran to the door. He returned a few minutes later and stood at the door, rather than make additional noise at the table.

"Of course, Deanna," said Reilly in a voice that could have sold a dead horse to a man running for his life. "As soon as we know, you will know."

There was a long soliloquy at the other end, which he bore with angelic patience. Finally, Stahl picked up his cell phone and dialled a number. A loud chirp emanated from Reilly's shirt pocket.

"Yes, I am afraid so," said Reilly. "Yes, I must. Thank you. Be well."

He shut off the phone with visible relief, smiled at Stahl and patted him on the shoulder. Stahl grinned and turned off his phone. The chirp in Reilly's pocket ceased.

Collins shook his head with bemusement, then scrambled to answer his own phone. He listened for a long time and then shut off the unit without a word.

"Two possible leads," he said to Reilly. "One is a fast ocean yacht that sailed from Sydney three days ago without orders from the owner. There is a love triangle between the owner, his wife and the skipper, however. The second is a fishing vessel that put to sea from Eden two days ago. It put off one crewman who says he didn't want to get involved with suspicious ongoings. He agonized about it for two days, then called us. They were to pick up one pudgy, blond-haired man in his early fifties who nominated a rendezvous with a large vessel just out of the heads. The boat was boarded an hour ago, and a man matching Morozov's description was apprehended. He has a heavy Russian accent."

"So how do you know that's Morozov?" asked Arnold with concern.

"I don't," replied Collins. "But his description matches, down to a faded scar on left shoulder."

"That's not a given," said Stockley. "No one actually knows what Morozov looks like today. There are no recent pictures."

"There aren't any pictures, correct," said Collins angrily. "Your establishment lost the file, if you remember."

Stockley sighed heavily and made a gesture of surrender with manicured hands.

"Wait a minute," said Collins. He lifted the phone and thumbed a few buttons.

"Inspector MacArdle?" he asked urgently. "One more request. Could you email Marsden the photos of all the men from the trawler? Thank you."

He thumbed the phone and thought furiously. Then he dialled another number.

"Marsden," he said urgently. "Pictures from the trawler, right. Listen. Print them and bring them to the helicopter pad."

He closed the phone and stood up.

"I have to make a quick house call, gentlemen," he explained curtly. "It will take a few hours, and it can't be done any faster."

As he left, he caught Reilly staring at him with apprehension.

The helicopter landed into heavy crosswind, coming to rest next to the police 4WD, parked on the scraggly lawn not far from the farm house.

The elderly woman sat on her porch, long strands of grey hair blowing across her forehead. She eyed the noisy proceedings with patience of one who had seen all manner of vanity and one who had witnessed much waste of life's precious time.

Collins strode up the stairs and inclined his head in greeting. She acknowledged him with a passive stare.

"Mother," he said respectfully. "I need your help."

She nodded.

Collins knelt in front of her on the grubby veranda and opened the envelope.

"Your neighbour, the one missing. We are

still trying to find him. Is he in these pictures?"

The old woman stretched out a boney hand and took the bundle from his hand. She slid the pictures from the envelope and studied them one by one. Collins watched as she slid the photographs back inside and extended her hand to return the envelope to Collins.

He stared at her expectantly. She emphatically shook her head.

Collins stood up, inhaling sharply. He took a few steps away from the veranda and turned, staring at the low hills covered with scrub as he thought. He looked down at the wooden pile and noticed the axe, deeply embedded in the chopping block. On the ground nearby he saw a rusty wood saw, its blade broken in two.

Collins turned back to the porch, extracting his wallet.

"Thank you, Mother," he told her, passing her a thin bundle of notes. She glanced at it impassively and shook her head with a light smile.

"Here, Mother," he pressed the money into her hand. "Buy yourself a new saw. A cold winter is coming."

###

Collins walked towards the scanner, holding

out his hands with irritation. He passed through without breaking stride and went into the briefing room without collecting his belongings.

"The New Zealanders are on the way to the second vessel," Hawthorne told him. "It's just out of the range of their helicopters, and it will take four to six hours to board."

Collins shrugged tiredly.

"We can wait," he replied.

"Maybe not," said Hawthorne. "We may have a problem."

Collins stared at him expectantly.

"The sub," said Hawthorne. "It submerged an hour ago."

Collins half-ran to the wall, where a large operation chart was stretched over a hastily erected stand.

There were only two red flags on the chart now. One marked the sub's last known location. A little distance away was the other, which marked the location of a fast ocean yacht. That much was known from satellite images.

Collins sighed heavily.

"Can we get assets there any faster?" he

asked forlornly.

Hawthorne shrugged his shoulders.

"We can detail a Sea King to fly over," he said uncertainly. It would have to drop men without being able to land - very risky."

"But a helicopter can stop the yacht," argued Collins. "Threaten to fire on it, surely, get men on board to drop sails, disable the engines."

"Yes, possibly," said Hawthorne. "We don't know what capability they have on board. But assuming it's a normal civilian vessel - yes, we could do that."

"Then we better get started," rasped Collins. "How fast could we get there?"

Hawthorne applied a ruler to the chart and did a few calculations in his head.

"If the boys on the frigate act quickly, they could get the Sea King within the hour. Give it two hours, depending on the wind, to reach the yacht. They would have to fly over, apprehend it and board, then the helicopter will have to fly on to land on one of the New Zealand vessels. Maybe there is a freighter nearby - that will make a safer landing."

He took out his phone and rapped out a string of orders.

"But here's the problem."

He applied the ruler to the chart again.

"Doing maximum speed, the sub can be there in two hours," he said. "By the way, the Russian government denied that the vessel is operating under orders. It's essentially a pirate mission."

"So could we fire on it?"

Hawthorne winced.

"They did not acquiesce to that request," he said reluctantly.

"Let's do what we can," Collins told him. "So long as we do it fast."

Morozov squinted into binoculars. It took him a while to see what the skipper's eagle eyes picked out some minutes before.

The crew exploded into action. Three squat, sunburnt men in yellow anoraks began to haul down the sails. The nose of the sleek vessel dropped into the heaving swell, slowing it instantly.

A few minutes later Morozov no longer needed binoculars to see a narrow silhouette protruding above the swell. It was moving towards them at some speed, judging by its wake in churning waters.

The yacht was now near-stationary, with all but the last few knots of forward speed remaining from its frantic drive towards the rendezvous point. The skipper tapped Morozov on the shoulder and jerked his thumb. Morozov turned around and saw a crewman gesture urgently from the stern.

He nodded his thanks to the skipper, who replied with a brief tilt of his head. Moving as instructed, Morozov grasped the guide rope with both hands and made his way aft. He was helped into an inflatable boat, which immediately reversed into the heaving sea. The crewman with faded blonde moustache amid a tanned face waited until they were clear and threw the motor into forward gear. Morozov lurched onto his knees as the inflatable raced away from the yacht.

A little distance ahead the submarine surfaced above the waves, foaming water surging against its gleaming black sides. A hatch opened on top of the tower, and two men in orange survival suits appeared amid the railing. One threw a broad rope ladder into the water.

The radio that hung around the crewman's neck squawked, and he raised it to his ear. Whatever was said, his expression changed to fright, and he gunned the motor. He turned to look over his shoulder briefly, and Morozov looked up to scan the horizon.

The cloud was still relatively high, and he could easily see the gleaming dot in the sky. It was approaching with obvious speed, leaving no doubt about its intentions.

The inflatable ran into the submarine with excessive speed, and Morozov fell face down into the salty puddle on the rubber deck. He felt the crewman jerk him upright, towards the rope ladder with great force. Adrenaline surged as he heard a loud ripping sound that a distant part of his brain acknowledged as heavy-calibre fire. As he scrambled up the ladder, he saw the rounds slice the water a little distance away from the inflatable.

"Davai! Davai!" strong hands hauled him up the last metre of the ladder and propelled him down, into the safety of the tower. He vaguely registered the rope ladder being dropped on top of him, wooden rungs lashing his back. He kept climbing down until there was nowhere left to go and came to rest on the metal deck wet with ocean water. Only then did it occur to him that he just heard his native language, spoken live, for the first time in three decades. There was a spasm in his throat.

A hawk-nosed, thin man in creased blue overalls strode up and studied Morozov's wet countenance, light contempt playing on his bloodless lips.

"You better be worth all this," he told him with a slight Baltic accent. "We are diving as fast as we can, but it won't be safe for a while. That helicopter clearly had no orders to attack, but they might change their mind and send one with torpedoes and a magnetic detector. We will go deep and change course, but they easily find us for at least another hour."

"Why are you telling me this?" asked Morozov hoarsely.

"Act important and aloof. You did not bring any equipment that looks worth dying for, so you are at least a general, understand?"

Morozov understood and nodded slowly.

"Discipline is not what it used to be," skipper curved his mouth in contempt. "Do not talk to any of my men - just 'where's the toilet' and 'thanks'. It's a long voyage, and you will need to be careful."

He walked away without awaiting the reply.

The dive siren sounded, and Morozov felt the submarine accelerate. The men in survival suits returned, stowed the ladder and walked away. Other crewmen came towards him with heavy blankets, into which he was wrapped for warmth.

Stiff-legged and nauseous, he was led down

the dimly lit corridor lined with pipes and cables as the vessel began to gather speed and dive. Morozov heard the hull creak as the vessel reached safe depth.

He was taken into cramped quarters and stood in front of a vent blowing hot air. Someone slapped him on the shoulder and told him to strip off the dripping clothes.

At that point Morozov began to shiver uncontrollably.

###

Collins filled the chair, not caring that his gut protruded from a crumpled and soiled white shirt. His tie was loose and askew, and he was aware of a number of odours, none of them flattering to his person.

Which did not matter any longer.

"What is it that you think you are doing?" asked Stahl with feigned curiosity. Reilly was past acting, noted Collins with satisfaction - the kindly round face with a shock of greying blonde hair was now a pale green mask.

"I've just finished with the entire business," said Collins leisurely. "But before I officially enter retirement, I decided to come here and give you an ultimatum."

"Indeed," spat Stahl with contempt.

"Keep quiet, you piece of shit," exploded Collins. "Not another word, or I will arrest you both, whatever the consequences."

He studied the shocked expressions.

"Yes, I can do that," he continued. "Maybe you will get off and maybe you won't."

"Klimov has disappeared," said Reilly hoarsely. "Without his evidence you have nothing."

Collins nodded.

"Maybe Klimov disappeared. But maybe he might resurface after attending to urgent personal business. His wife died in the outbreak, you know. His disappearance may well be temporary."

He waited, but there was no reply.

"That's not all," he explained. "You see, I also have this."

He extracted a carelessly folded bundle of papers from his inner jacket pocket and threw them across, hitting Stahl on the face. Stahl flinched and made no attempt to retrieve the paper from the floor, staring at Collins.

Reilly bent down and placed the papers on his desk. He opened them with shaking hands, and Collins was rewarded with a sharp intake of breath.

Stahl reached over to clutch the document. He read the first few lines and shook his head with dismay.

"Personally, I never got on with ASIO," said Collins. "Slimy bunch, and that Deakin kid doesn't belong there, I say. As soon as he put two and two together, he found the requisition documents, made illicit copies and got them over to me. Cut the lining of his suit to get them out of the building, just like the spies of old. Cool customer, that young man."

He looked around and nodded affirmatively.

"Don't bother looking for him, by the way," he added. "He won't be surfacing until the whole deal is over."

Reilly cleared his throat.

"Your ultimatum," he said tentatively.

"Oh yes," Collins startled, as if reminded. "Yes. You two will go. You are about to have a minor stroke, Mr Reilly."

"That amounts to a coup d'etat," said Reilly flatly.

"I am sure you are right," replied Collins generously. "But it is so much better than being arrested, charged, tried - even if you won't get convicted. I would much prefer to go to the media, have you investigated and stung by various wasps for the rest of your lives, not to mention wiping your party off the political scene forever - but unlike you, I am a patriot. I don't want my country to be known as the place where elections are rigged by foreign cut-throats at the behest of the highest bidder."

Reilly swallowed hard, thought for a few moments and nodded.

"You will take your pet reptile with you," continued Collins without looking in Stahl's direction. "It goes without saying that neither of you will ever resurface in public life."

Reilly nodded quickly.

"There will be no speeches, knighthoods, academic posts, diplomatic appointments - nothing," repeated Collins emphatically. "No memoirs, no lobby jobs, no company directorships - neither of you gets a single drop of gravy, you understand?"

Reilly nodded again.

"I will need my pension," he said hoarsely.

Collins waved his hand in dismissal.

"You will need it to stay silent," he said in a more conciliatory tone. "I expect you to settle in a small town and clip roses. Have your port or three in the evening, sleep as well as you can - and keep your mouth shut. As for the reptile, I rather think emigration is in order."

He turned to Stahl and fixed him with a policeman's stare.

"You will go to a quiet Third World country where brave reporters don't go because they get diarrhoea every time they order a latte. Do what you please, but stay there for two years, then find a permanent home overseas. UK is far enough. In the interest of your health, I opine that you should never cross the equator again."

Stahl moved to say something, but Reilly waved him off.

"Remember," said Collins. "It is not about a threat of prosecution. No. If the extent of your involvement becomes public, you can expect a bullet anywhere you go. One hundred and twenty-six totally innocent citizens lost their lives because of your scam - that's not counting the dead from the strike. We have pretty strict gun laws in our country, but I am sure that one of the grieving relatives can get his hands on a firearm."

Collins nodded with a wry smile.

"You will be foolish to expect official protection," he added. "Foolish indeed."

Reilly and Stahl sat still, waiting for him to continue.

"I take it we are in complete agreement?" asked Collins, not expecting a reply. "Of course we are. Of course."

He dug deeper in his jacket pocket and tossed a business card on the table.

"You will begin to feel unwell tonight," he told Reilly. "Your dedicated staff will call this excellent man, who will admit you to a private clinic for urgent tests in the early hours of tomorrow morning. The results will indicate that you are at risk of a big stroke, and you will act on his recommendation and retire, all without leaving the hospital bed or giving interviews."

He looked at them significantly.

"Well, that's pretty much all," he concluded. "Thank you for your rapt attention. I'll be going now - need to whisper a word or two in Dave Stockley's ear before the day is done."

Collins rose to his feet with some difficulty and smiled.

"You might bump into old Dave on the golf course, once the doctor clears you to perform mild exertion. Early retirement seems in fashion today."

Air brakes hissed and emitted unhealthy clanging noises, but the massive rig stopped opposite the church façade as required.

"Christ has arisen, Father," said the driver joyfully.

"Verily arisen," replied Klimov making a sign of the cross over the driver's shaven head. The broad cheeks bearing a collection of brawling scars creased in a sincere smile. It was Easter.

Klimov made another sign of the cross over

the rig's instrument panel.

"Go with thanks, my son."

He resisted the urge to shake hands and opened the door, jumping to the distant ground nimbly. That manoeuvre nearly resulted in tragedy as he tripped over his cassock, but Klimov salvaged his balance and pressed home the heavy door, patting it for emphasis.

The diesel monster growled and belched filth into the dusky sky. Klimov made another sign of the cross in the wake of the overloaded trailer and began to walk towards the cemetery gates.

He was pretty sure that he could not be recognized by his own mother, had the good lady come down from Communist heaven, to guide him through that pale Moscow dusk.

The dark hair was gone, leaving a shiny skull adorned with the neat headgear of the Orthodox priest. In compensation, he now wore a short beard with drooping moustache, dyed greying blonde. He wore thick glasses in an aged plastic frame. Only a very experienced observer would notice that the lenses were of plain glass, with no corrective value whatsoever.

He wore a plain dark tracksuit under the cassock, with black walking boots that neither detracted from his costume nor impeded running. A worn wallet hung from his neck contained a passable Ukrainian passport and a small bundle of greasy notes - roubles, grivnas and dollars. Far greater funds were available upon presentation of a memorized combination of numbers to any branch of Deutsche Bank, with no hint of such capability on his person.

Klimov chose to go unarmed - bar a weapon that even a seasoned investigator would fail to suspect. His cross was solid steel, long enough to serve as a dagger - the lowest arm was sharpened to a chisel-like edge. God willing, it was heavy enough and sharp enough to penetrate someone's ribs in time of need. The chain was imitation silver, and the weapon could be torn from his neck with minimal effort.

He turned into the cemetery and began to walk along the memorized path as dusk began to deepen. The city noise had died away, replaced by the whisper of a spring breeze and birdsong. Klimov felt a sting in his nose and tears began to form on his eyes. He walked on steadily, salty drops rolling down his cheeks.

He took up position some distance away from his destination, kneeling next to a black slab marking the resting place of someone wealthy. Any observer would size him up as a youngish priest praying at a nominated grave, possibly at the behest of a guilty relative. Klimov's lips moved in silent recitation, and every now and again he made the sign of the cross over the black marble.

Behind bottle glasses his eyes darted around, scanning for signs of surveillance. There were none, he was sure - only a few elderly people scurried by, in a rush to leave the cemetery before dark.

At nightfall Klimov began to move. Just a block away from his goal he stole behind a bush and froze, listening and almost smelling for hostile presence.

Satisfied that he was alone, he resumed movement in a crouch, guided by dim moonlight. As darkness fell and night chill penetrated the cassock, he finally reached his goal.

It was possible to read the gold-leafed inscription once the moon emerged from a break in the clouds, and tears streamed down his worn face. He knelt in the damp grass and pressed his forehead into cold stone, searing his grief into Raisa's grave.

Eventually the tears ran dry. Klimov scrambled onto his feet and nimbly disappeared into the bushes, running away in near-silence. Closer to the exit he slowed down, wiped his tears and began to walk at normal pace. He exited the cemetery, crossed the busy road and marched into a narrow alley, where he could not be followed without his knowledge. To his mild surprise there was no tail - he walked down the maze of alleys between ancient apartment blocks all alone. A few dubious creatures of the night passed him on the way to the nearest Metro station, but none challenged him as he walked onto the escalator and descended into the crowded station.

At an observation post in the cemetery Pogrebiev, now a major, lowered the night goggles and gave his face a good rub.

"Was that anything?" asked his assistant, a hard-faced young man perched next to him inside an old vault.

Pogrebiev shook his head as if dispelling an apparition.

"Nothing," he replied. "What a ridiculous mission, anyway. As if a professional like Klimov would risk his life to come here, after what he did. Take over, would you? I need a smoke."

"You will be met here," the skipper stabbed a long, boney finger into the chart.

Morozov studied the dense isoclines on the topographic map with distaste.

"By whom?"

"An armoured column, no less," replied the

captain. "It's a nasty shore these days - no one really owns it. No man's land, even into to the mountains."

Morozov nodded.

"It will be good to see daylight," he said absently. After six weeks at sea, mostly under a vow of silence, he meant that most sincerely.

The captain affected a total lack of interest.

"We will be at destination in twenty minutes," he replied, pressing the intercom button. A sailor in greasy overalls appeared at the door of the cabin. "Escort sir to the tower. He wants fresh air."

The sailor saluted briefly and backed out of the door without a change of expression. Morozov turned to walk down the corridor, shadowed by the crewman.

Climbing the rungs of the tower, he greedily inhaled the salty breeze but was disappointed to find the sea in total darkness. He was helped aboard another inflatable boat, and this time there was no rush. The submarine remained stationary as the inflatable took off, approaching the distant shore slowly and quietly. Morozov breathed the air with relish.

Once they were through the gentle surf the engine was cut altogether, and the inflatable drifted the last few metres of its voyage, rattling on the shingle as it slid onto the beach. Morozov rose to his feet and cautiously stepped overboard, his feet sinking into wet stones.

Six figures silently emerged from dark boulders, and one of them slid the hood of a camouflage anorak off his helmet. He stepped towards Morozov and saluted.

"Lieutenant Bogrov. I am General Pertzov's representative," he whispered into Morozov's ear. "The area is not secure, and we need to move silently and quickly. Are you able to do that?"

Morozov nodded once.

"Follow me closely," said Bogrov. He made a circling motion with his hand, and three figures ran up the path away from the shore. More arose from the stones to follow at a discrete distance.

They climbed a small cliff into the forest, Morozov puffing mightily. He tried to exercise during the voyage, but the very air made him ill. The pervasive odours of machine oil, ozone and sweat made it hard for him to breathe through his mouth. There was no escape from that stench, and he simply stopped exercising, breathing through a half-blocked nose instead.

They were now deep in the pines, moving along uneven ground at a steady pace.

Morozov revelled in the pine-scented breeze that blew across his sweat-covered face. As the slope began to even out, they slowed down the pace, then one of the men leading the party motioned them to stop. Someone's hand pushed Morozov into low ferns.

He discerned three large shapes in the low undergrowth. One of the men in the lead extracted a radio handset from the pocket of his combat jacket and thumbed the button at the side.

"Nightingale nearing nest."

There was a brief silence, then the radio crackled into life.

"Nest warm and waiting."

They ran towards the shapes, and Morozov now realized that they were tanks - larger and lower than the T-72's of his youth. He was guided under one of them, where the bottom hatch was opened and rested on the ground. He was helped into the interior of the machine, backlit with red light that did not interfere with night vision.

Engines growled into life, and the machine shot forward, gathering speed with a whine of its turbine. The crewman who helped him inside handed Morozov a large headset, indicating that it went over both ears.

"It's not safe," he told Morozov through the intercom. "Reports of fighting in this sector in the last few days. Not too much here that can threaten us, but we are ordered to take no chances with your safety."

Morozov nodded. He was mildly nauseated by the tank rocking on its suspension and suddenly overcome by apathy - after travelling half-way around the world by various uncomfortable and illegal means, he was desperate for a sleep in a warm bed that stood firmly on solid ground.

Anxiety gave way to fatigue. Morozov rested his head against the greasy bulkhead and fell asleep.

The nap was frequently interrupted by the tank jolting over deep ruts. Then the engine growled abruptly, and the machine shuddered as brakes were applied with no regard for consequences. Morozov's head slammed into the bulkhead, and he sat up in irritation.

The complaint died on his lips as he saw the breach of the cannon being opened with some urgency. The commander turned towards him and began to say something about staying low. Then the machine appeared to leap into the air.

Headphones saved Morozov's eardrums from bursting, but he was still deafened and screamed in pain, clutching his ears. The next explosion ripped open the turret, and he was thrown with great force against hard metal. There was rapid machine gun fire overhead as he passed out.

Large bearded men emerged from the forest, moving in a fast, crouching run. They eliminated survivors who tried to fire on them from the tanks.

Once the last of the gunfire died down, strong arms reached into the mutilated hull. Morozov's limp body was jerked up and thrown on the ground without ceremony.

The leader of the raiding party handed his assault rifle to the next man and leaned down, shining a torch on Morozov's face. He extracted a photograph from the pocket of his tunic and lifted Morozov's head by the sparse hair, carefully comparing the face to the photograph.

Satisfied, the Chechen handed the torch to his subordinate and let Morozov's head drop to the ground. Morozov moaned and opened his eyes.

A very large knife with a razor-keen edge slid from the shoulder sheath and flashed in the moonlight. It sliced through blood vessels in Morozov's throat and completed the arc of its swing without slowing. The Chechen jumped back to avoid being splashed with blood and stood aside until the dark fountain subsided.

The body contorted, then fell back to the ground, forever free of fear.

The second man extracted a thick plastic bag from his pocket. His leader bent down, lifted the body by the bloody shirt and sawed off the head with a few rhythmic strokes of the blade. He lifted it by its gaping teeth and dropped it into the proffered plastic bag. Wiping his hands on the grass, he took back his assault rifle and smiled broadly.

"Allah be praised," he said loudly.

"Praised be He," came the reply in a perfect chorus.

###

"Eat that!" yelled Collins. He broke the shotgun and replaced two smoking shells. "Crawling deadshits. Fuck you!"

It was a bad year for snakes. The heat and the drought forced the wretched creatures into the sovereign territory of their worst enemy. The grass was mowed almost bare, and the swimming pool was religiously covered at dusk, to the chagrin of patrons craving its cool waters - for even after dark it was uncomfortably hot.

The snakes kept coming in from the bush in record numbers, and Collins maintained high vigil. It was almost time to fence off the motel's lawns and get sheep, whose mindless meanderings kept the reptiles at bay. But that move looked less than promising now that the grass was gone for the summer, and Collins had no choice but to march around in overalls and gumboots in searing heat, a hessian sack draped over the shotgun for decorum. The ammunition was hand-loaded to minimize noise, but it was hardly a welcoming look.

Collins bent down to what was left of the snake and snatched up the headless ruin on the end of the barrel. He threw the dripping remains into the bushes and hoped that the goannas he was feeding would begin to take care of business without his involvement. Even in retirement there was no escape from a basic reality of reptiles consuming other reptiles - the current problem being that they did not consume with sufficient speed.

By now he was dizzy with the heat, and it was time to disrobe. He shambled back to the office and reached behind the counter to flick a switch. A roller door began to rumble nearby, and Collins entered the welcome coolness of the garage, stripping off the overalls and shedding his gumboots into the doorless closet. He was in need of a good wash.

Now barefoot, clad only in shorts and a torn singlet, he went outside. There he lifted the nozzle of the garden hose over his head and turned the tap. He sprinkled the sweat off his body, muttering that it was time for a beer.

It was a quiet day - all units stood empty, and the cleaners had long left. Kookaburras rampaged in the trees across the river, earning a muffled obscenity in their direction. They were supposed to catch the snakes first and laugh later.

Collins retrieved a beer from an old fridge in the office and popped the lid, savouring the sting of bitter foam on his parched mouth.

"Is there one for me?" asked a slightly sarcastic voice.

Collins wheeled around, spilling beer from the can. Klimov was leaning on the office wall with a wry smile.

He lost weight, noticed Collins, and there was a rim of white skin where he recently shaved off a beard. A stubble of greying black hair covered the skull. His clothes were a non-descript attire of the summer vacationer - faded jeans and a light T-shirt. He even wore sandals, albeit of a heavy type favoured by backpackers.

Collins stared at him as smile replaced alarm. They shook hands, then Collins reached into the fridge, retrieving the entire slab of beer cans from within.

"To your new enterprise," Klimov raised his can in toast. "I approve."

They sat down in the shade where ferns grew profusely under the carport. Collins carefully studied the ground before sitting down, but no reptilian visitors were in evidence.

Penny wandered across the motel lawn, carrying a dented plastic bowl in her jaws. She dropped the bowl next to Collins and flopped down in the shade.

Collins poured the remainder of his can into the bowl and opened another. Klimov drank deeply and belched into his fist.

"Did you get him?" asked Collins.

Klimov drank again and set the empty can on the rusty wrought-iron table.

"I did," he replied blandly.

Collins nodded.

"I flew into Ukraine," explained Klimov. "Bought a false passport and travelled into the Caucasus. After some inconvenience and a few adventures, I was able to meet with Imam Ramzanov."

"Who?"

"The leader of the Chechen resistance – until Pertzov gets his hands on him."

Collins sipped his beer; Klimov bent down and popped the next can. He drained the contents in a single long gulp and crushed the can in his fist.

"It's very hot," he said apologetically. "So I met with Ramzanov. He listened to me with great care, and I cannot fault his attention or hospitality. It is amazing how reasonable enemies can unite against someone who abandoned all reason and restraint."

Collins waited patiently.

"I calculated the duration of the submarine voyage with some accuracy," continued Klimov immodestly. "My estimate was wrong by just three days. Just as Ramzanov's thugs began to exhibit some impatience, what did we see through night goggles? Up floated the submarine, over came the boat with Morozov and down the mountain came a tank detachment from Pertzov. Precisely as I predicted. The Chechens ogled me as if I was some kind of unholy prophet."

He reached for the next can.

"Ramzanov's men wiped out the column."

Collins sipped his beer without comment.

"I stayed in his camp long enough to view Morozov's head the morning," Klimov told him. "It ended up on a spike outside Ramzanov's tent. I wanted to stay longer and watch it rot, but there was always a chance that Ramzanov may change his mind about being a gracious host. All kinds of concerns played on my mind - that he may decide to silence me, to force me into his employ because of my talents – or even, heaven forbid, enslave me sexually."

Collins laughed involuntarily and shook his head.

"Why not?" asked Klimov indignantly. "I am, after all, a very presentable man for my age."

"If you say so," rumbled Collins, downing the last of his beer. He let out a gargantuan burp and reached for the depleted stock of cans.

"So it was time to go," said Klimov, his tone turning grim. "I took a little detour to pay my respects to my wife's final resting place."

Collins nodded in sympathy.

"I know how that feels," he said softly.

"Now I do as well," Klimov nodded with sadness. "I took some risk, but contrary to expectations, I was not apprehended at the cemetery. I am not sure why they were so lax - my superior would want to skin me. Very much."

"Perhaps for once you did not all think alike," observed Collins. "Or maybe they were just short-staffed."

Klimov put down his beer and contemplated that statement.

"Difficult to imagine," he said sceptically. "In any case, I am back. I decided to stay here under a false identity."

"Like Morozov?"

"Indeed. Maybe I can have his old cabin in the bush. I solemnly promise that I had not brought any lethal viruses."

"That cabin has been sold," replied Collins instantly. "But I have a better offer."

Klimov inclined his head in attention.

"First a question," said Collins. Klimov looked at him in expectation.

"What happens to Pertzov?"

"Nothing, sadly. He is untouchable."

"That stinks, don't you think?"

"Yes, but that's just one of such smells in Russia," Klimov sighed and drained the last drops from the can. "But I wouldn't envy Pertzov - you see, bandits like that can only expect loyalty so long as they get results. Now, his campaign has been running out of steam -

as do all such campaigns in that part of the world. The virus was his great hope - without it he can expect a quagmire. Sooner or later his failures will begin to outweigh his successes, and Pertzov will wind up in the gutter with a subordinate's bullet in the back of his head."

"What about the facility?" asked Collins. "I mean, where that horrid thing was made."

"Rebirth Island? Dismantled in 1992. The equipment and virus samples were moved to more secure places. They were guarded with some paranoia even before Pertzov's stunt, but now they will be impossible to come near. The President himself would have to fight to get anywhere near them. Officially, you see, they hadn't existed after the bioweapons treaty we signed with the Yanks, way back in the Soviet days."

Collins shook his head with disgust.

"Let's get you asylum," he said pensively. "Not much of a life hiding like that forever."

"That would be preferable," agreed Klimov. "I don't think they would risk another messy expedition if I came out of hiding. My old comrades, I mean."

"My old comrades could even mention it to them," mused Collins. "The undesirability of it. Yes, I should think that everyone would want this file to stay closed."

"Hopefully. And then?"

"And then," said Collins gruffly. "We will see what happens. Say, I know you impersonated all sorts of people in your long career."

"So I did. Lately a priest - is there a local vacancy?"

"I wouldn't know," rumbled Collins. "Not my scene. The question is - have you ever impersonated anyone running a country motel?"

Klimov smiled, but his eyes fixed Collins with an attentive stare.

"The paperwork," explained Collins. "It drives me spare - but you look like the type who would thrive on that job. Plus the odd bit of security work - I don't think that would bother you either."

"It will be an honour," replied Klimov solemnly.

"It's very quiet out here," said Collins apologetically. "But peaceful - no trouble of any kind."

"Don't worry," replied Klimov, rising from his seat and looking away. "I crave nothing but peace. I've had enough excitement for many consecutive lifetimes."

He turned towards Collins and smiled, rapidly blinking moisture from his eyes.

"Easiest decision I ever had to make," he reported, extending his hand.

IBE
1991-2010